BLOOD DEBT

KINGDOM OF BLOOD #1

CALLIE ROSE

Copyright © 2021 by Callie Rose

All rights reserved.

No part of this book may be reproduced in any form or by any electronic or mechanical means, including information storage and retrieval systems, without written permission from the author.

This is a work of fiction. Names, characters, organizations, and incidents are either products of the author's imagination or used fictitiously. Any resemblance to actual persons, living or dead, is purely coincidental.

For updates on my upcoming releases and promotions, sign up for my reader newsletter! I promise not to bite (or spam you).

CALLIE ROSE NEWSLETTER

We are each our own devil, and we make this world our hell.

— **OSCAR WILDE**

CHAPTER ONE

I hear there are places in this world where the rain washes the dirt out of the sky and leaves everything feeling fresh and clean.

Not here.

The rain is as dirty as the air, and the water only serves to accentuate the pungent destitution of the streets below. Rotting wood and rotting flesh fill my nose with warning scents.

More human victims, or just dead rats?

I brush the thought aside, narrowing my focus as I skirt around weak spots on the rooftop I'm traversing. It would be stupid as fuck to lose my life to a fall at this point. Losing it in a fight? That's a different story. I'm pretty sure that's how I'll go eventually.

Not tonight, though. Not this fight.

I heard the vamp making its kill, and that's one point

against the stupid fucker already. It's careless enough to let its victim scream. Not that there aren't plenty of other screams in this city on a nightly basis. This is Baltimore, after all. Screams happen. But screams that start with a gasp and end in a gurgle?

Those are unique.

Those are the screams of vampire food.

I'm watching the vamp run from above. He's dressed to blend in—gray sweats and a black hoodie. Most bloodsuckers don't really do the whole Renaissance thing with the way they dress, at least not above ground. What they do in their underground palace is a mystery to everybody but the poor souls stupid or unfortunate enough to get suckered into blood slavery. I couldn't tell you how many people that actually is, but if you've seen the missing persons statistics around here, you can make an educated guess.

He's heading for the Block. They all do eventually. There's something about strip clubs that draws them—probably all that excited blood flow and exposed flesh.

This will work to my advantage though.

There's a blind alley between here and there, right at the end of this row, where a busted fire escape dangles unexpectedly in the middle. I've ambushed more than a few creatures there and always had the upper hand. It's a loud alley anyway, and the rain gives me even more cover.

I reach the corner before he does and get into position. He's almost under me, looking back over his shoulder. He knows he's being stalked, he's just wrong about where the real predator is. From this perspective, I judge him to be about two hundred and fifty pounds of muscle on a five-foot nine-inch frame. I hope that means he'll move a little slower, but I'm not optimistic. I only have a second to process all of that before he's under me. I drop precisely, landing ass-to-chest with my thighs over each of his shoulders, knocking the wind out of him with the force of my twenty-foot drop.

"Heads up, asshole."

I whip out my blades, one in each hand, and go for his throat.

Before I can touch him, he's got his hand between my thighs, pressing outward to shove me off him. I curl my legs and kick off of his chest, knocking him back as I flip to land on my feet. His fangs gleam in the dull streetlights, and he growls savagely as he charges at me.

He's trying to get me in a headlock. I'm slippery, but he's strong. If he catches me, I'm done for.

I slip between his legs as he makes a grab for me, then turn and kick him squarely in the small of his back. He barely stumbles. Before I'm ready for the next attack, he's lunging for me, teeth out, eyes blazing, aiming for my waist. I duck sideways and then shove him, using his momentum to send him to the ground. Then I raise my booted foot and kick as hard as I can, curb-stomping his head before landing on his back with my knees.

"Aaaah!"

With a feral yell, he flips over, tossing me away like I weigh nothing, then charges at me again.

He's pissed. Off-balance. Out-of-control.

Just the way I like them.

In his rage, he leaves his throat open. In one smooth motion, I cross my curved blades, then uncross them with every ounce of strength I have at the exact moment that his throat is between them. Every fiber of his thick neck sends vibrations through my blades, his bones scraping like broken china on steel.

He doesn't make a sound.

He doesn't have the chance to.

His lifeless head falls to the ground, the snarl still frozen on his monstrous face. Within seconds, his head and torso both crumble to dust. Rain dribbles through the piles, turning them to mud, and that mud mixes with the common filth in the gutters.

One down. God knows how many to go.

I wipe the vampire's blood off my blades and slide them into their sheaths on my thighs. Vamps don't have as much blood as you'd expect, but what little they *do* have is hell on my weapons if it's allowed to sit.

My nerves are on high alert, my senses taking in every sound. The vampire was working alone when I found him, but these fuckers always end up in groups eventually. Unless I want to risk getting jumped and outnumbered, I'd better leave before any of his friends show up.

I shove my hands into my pockets and put my head down. My phone vibrates against my leg inside my pocket as I turn out of the alley, and I walk a little faster. I don't want to talk or make too much noise that close to my kill and risk giving my position away.

When I'm a few blocks away from the location of the dead vamp, I dig my phone out of my pocket and glance down at the screen. It's Nathan.

I don't know why the hell my brother is calling me at this time of night, but knowing Nate, it's nothing good.

"What's up?" I answer, glancing around at the rain-slicked streets and keeping my voice down.

"Mikka, I fucked up."

That's all it takes. Just those four fucking words. I can hear the panic in them, and it sets off every protective alarm bell in my body. I start sprinting toward the abandominium he's recently claimed as his apartment. It's only a few miles from here—and in this moment, I'm grateful as fuck for that.

"Did you OD?" My voice comes out choppy, and the phone bounces against my ear as I run.

"Nah—not yet—wish I did. I'm, um—I'm in a lot of trouble with a lot of people, Mikka. I had no choice. I had to do it."

"You had to do what?"

He sucks in a shaky breath. "You have to understand, sis. Please. I owed a lot of people a shitload of money. Bad people, very bad people. I—I know you don't have any left, or I would have asked you for help, I swear. I just had to call you to tell you before—before—"

He wheezes into the phone, like he can't make himself say any more.

My heart sinks like a stone into my belly. "Nathan, what the fuck did you do?"

"I sold myself," he says through a sob.

I slow my run, and my pulse seems to slow down along with my feet. "Are we talking dick sucking, or—?"

"Not like that." He lets out a sound that could be a sob or a laugh, I can't fucking tell. Maybe it's both. "I sold myself to the vampires. As a blood tribute. It was the only way, you have to believe me."

Time freezes around me. The darkness seems to swallow his words up, stealing them and muffling them in inky black.

Blood tribute.

My own brother has sold himself to the goddamn vampires.

"I don't believe you," I force out, my throat tight. "You'd never be that fucking stupid. You could have come to me. Why didn't you come to me? Nathan? Nathan!"

I jerk the phone away from my face to find myself

talking to my home screen. The call's already gone dead from his side.

My stomach feels like it's full of battery acid, and I blink at the phone as if it has the power to rewind time and undo everything he just said.

Shit. I'm too far away. There are no fucking cabs around here, and I'll never get there in time if all I do is run.

I start running anyway.

CHAPTER TWO

I'm running and dialing, listening to the phone ring until the voicemail picks up, and dialing again. I'm soaked in sweat and filthy rain, and his building is still at least two miles away. I need a motherfucking cab. There aren't a whole lot of those in this neighborhood, but luck's on my side for once. After about ten minutes of all-out sprinting, I see a cab pull around the corner up ahead of me. I flag it down and hop in, shouting the address at the driver.

"You have fare?" he asks, glaring suspiciously.

Jesus. Of fucking course. I'm covered in blood and mud and whatever other dirt was in that alley. I look like a bum, so I can't really blame the guy. I pull a small wad of cash out of my pocket and shove it at him.

"There. Drive, dammit!"

"Yeah, yeah. All right."

With another skeptical look at me, he turns around and

grips the wheel. But fortunately, he seems as eager to get me where I'm going as I am to get there. I'm sure it's for different reasons—he probably just wants me to stop dripping blood and dirt on his back seat—but I don't give a fuck.

He slams on the gas and peels out.

Baltimore swirls around me, the good smashed against the awful and the ugly, and all of it nothing more than a front for supernatural predators. People like to talk about how bad the drug problem is in this city—but shit, they'd all be shooting up too if they knew they were living on top of a goddamn vampire nest. Even the ones who say they don't believe in vampires have seen some shit they can't explain and lived some shit they want to forget.

After what feels like forever, the cab screeches to a stop in front of my brother's shitty-ass building. The lower windows are all boarded up, the steps are crumbling around the edges, and the door is hanging at a stupid angle. Upstairs, candles flicker in some of the windows. The smell of urine is overwhelming. I can't tell if it's human or animal, which means it's probably both. There's no running water here, no electricity, and it's full of rats—but it's shelter from the elements and the cops don't have the manpower to clear it out. Nathan thinks he was lucky to find it. I think Nathan's been so low for so long he doesn't remember what luck looks like.

Since the entryway door is busted anyway, I don't even

bother trying the derelict panel of buzzers. Instead, I just burst in and race up the stairs, dodging random puddles of various liquids and the occasional passed-out junkie. Nathan's apartment door is cracked open too, and I shove my way in, hands going to my weapons, ready to fight.

"Nathan!" I call, my voice hoarse. "Nathan! Where the fuck are you?"

The living room—if you can call it that—is empty. So is the bedroom and the dry, grimy bathroom. I scream for him again, not caring if I'm waking his neighbors, but I know it's pointless.

He's gone.

I'm too late.

He must've called me right before he left, probably because he *knew* I'd try to stop him.

Ice twists through my belly. I'm shaking, and my face is wet with tears, even though I can't feel them falling. Shit. I haven't cried in a long time, and I'm pissed off that I'm crying now.

Dammit, Nathan. What the hell could be so bad that you had to go to the fucking vampires?

He's got piles of paper stacked around the place, mostly scrap paper with notes scribbled all over in his slanted, erratic handwriting. Shopping lists are mixed up with horse's names, and random dates and dollar amounts are scribbled all over everything. Crouching on the floor of his living room, I riffle through pile after pile until I come across a piece of paper with a phone number written in a beautiful, old-fashioned hand. Of course it's written in red. Vampires are dramatic bitches. Beside it, *Call Mikka* is circled twice.

"Okay, but what did you *do*?" I mutter. "What the hell did you get yourself into, Nathan?"

When I flip the paper over, my heart sinks. It's an itemized bill from a bookie, totaling hundreds of thousands of dollars. At the bottom, in Nathan's handwriting, is a dollar amount for slightly more, with *Blood Tribute Minimum Bid* written beside it.

My hands start to shake even worse, and the scrawled note blurs in my vision as I blink away new tears. I put the paper down before my trembling fingers can accidentally rip it.

"You idiot," I growl, grinding my fists into the filthy carpet. "You absolute fucking idiot!"

I should have known. I should have stopped this. Certain people in this town talk about vampires the way other people talk about loan sharks or hooking. If you can't pay your bill, they'll point at those goddamn monsters and say *look, I know you're not really trying, because if you were, you would have explored* all *the options*. I should have seen this coming, dammit. Nathan already told me he sold sex once to pay a bill, and I've already bailed him out from under a loan shark before. This is the final stop on the debt train, but I never thought he would go this far. Never.

My brain is a chaotic mess, and I grind my teeth together, trying to organize my thoughts.

Think, dammit. Come on, Mikka. Focus.

The note says minimum bid, so he's clearly not selling himself directly. He must've pledged himself to the auction house—the place people go to offer themselves up to the vampires of Baltimore as "tributes."

I've never been inside it, but I know where it is. Downtown, there's a bar. Behind the bar is a strip club, which is a front for the whorehouse in the basement. Behind that basement is another, larger basement which used to be attached to a museum. The museum doesn't exist anymore, but the security measures are still in place. It's impossible to get in unseen—and, from what I can tell, it's impossible to get out at all.

So, fuck it, I won't even try to get in without being seen. I'll do the exact opposite.

I won't be the first woman to offer myself up to the vampires willingly, not by a long shot. It happens all the time. All I have to do is play dumb and pretend I've watched too many sparkle-emo movies.

I suppress a shudder as I think about what happens next. If they pick me as a tribute—which they fucking better—I'll be taken to the palace. Or *fortress*, whatever you want to call it. You'd be right either way. I've never seen the inside of it, but I've been down in the old paved-over parts of Baltimore enough times to know exactly where it is. It's impenetrable from the outside. A massive high-rise made of steel and bulletproof glass sits on top of it, and vampires patrol the sealed perimeter. Waste that smells like spilled blood and old wine trickles between grates too small for a mouse to get through, and too strong to break with anything short of a natural disaster. The only way in is to be brought in.

And the only way to do *that* is to sell myself.

Wiping my hand over my face, I look around the rest of Nathan's apartment. I already know I'm going to save him, that I'll do whatever it takes to get him out of the vampires' hold in one piece. It's what I do, whenever I can. Save him. I haven't had much luck saving him from himself, but I'll be damned if I don't rescue him from these vampires.

Scrambling to my feet, I grab the note again and stuff it in my back pocket. Then I glance around the dilapidated space. If Nathan has anything worth anything in this apartment, I should take it back to my place for safekeeping. Knowing this city, his apartment will be occupied again by tomorrow night.

"And he's never coming back here," I mutter under my breath, my nails digging into my palms as I curl my hands into fists. "Never. I'll make him live with me again, whether he likes it or not. I can make it work this time, I know I can."

Before he moved into this shithole, I offered to let him stay with me, like he's done from time to time in the past.

But he refused, no matter how much I begged and cajoled. He promised me this dump was just going to be a temporary housing solution, a place he could stay rent-free for a little bit while he sorted some things out.

He told me he didn't want to be a burden, and I eventually gave in and let him have his way. And this is the fucking result of that.

Blowing out a breath, I shove down my anger, guilt, and sadness, focusing on the task at hand. I need to grab anything valuable and get back to my place to change out of my hunting clothes. Every second counts.

In the tiny bedroom, I spot a framed picture hanging on the wall over his bed. The frame is the nicest thing in the apartment, and I'm pretty sure it must've cost him a whole dollar. It's a picture of the two of us from ten years ago, at one of the "Family Forever" picnics the foster families in our neighborhood used to throw. Officially, they did them so that separated siblings could maintain relationships.

Unofficially, it was an auction. Foster moms would literally sit there and trade kids. Some of them wanted docile kids. Some wanted kids who could hold their own with the bullies at school. Some wanted hard workers, and some wanted girls at risk of pregnancy because hell, two checks were better than one. Didn't matter to me and Nathan, though. We were just happy to see each other. I was fourteen in this picture, which would have made Nathan fifteen.

I press my fingers to the cold glass over his face. That smile, that *real* smile, the one that reached his green eyes and made the corners crinkle—I haven't seen it in so long. Not since that summer, in fact. One year after this picture was taken, I moved to a house on the good side of Federal Hill, with a family who assumed my brother was bad news just because he was older than me. They stopped letting me see him. I fought it, but there was only so much I could do at that point.

So I threw myself into building skills. Knife-throwing, swordsmanship, martial arts... anything I could get my hands on. Since I was living with a relatively wealthy family at the time, they indulged all of my extracurricular requests—as long as I also agreed to do ballet and gymnastics. At the time, I thought those two things were useless, but once I was actually out fighting vampires, I found out how priceless those skills really are.

Nathan went the other way. He never got lucky enough to match with a family who were interested in helping him deal with our parents' deaths. Without me around, he went looking for his own ways to mend his broken heart. Someone gave him a needle and told him to stitch his heart back together with that. It didn't work, obviously, but it masked the pain enough to keep him hooked.

Then there was the alcohol and women and gambling. It's real easy for a tall boy to be treated as a man around here, for better or for worse. In Nathan's case, it was worse. At seventeen, he'd seen and done things that no grown-ass adult should even know about, let alone a kid.

When I graduated and got out of the system, I tried to take him with me. My foster parents set me up in an apartment and let me choose between college or having my bills paid for a year. I chose the latter, which they were happy about—it was cheaper, after all—and I brought Nathan home to live with me. I thought I could save him back then, I really did. But he just kept getting worse and worse. I dealt with it for as long as I could. At least, that's what I keep telling myself.

"I'm not going to let you down again," I promise the smiling boy in the photograph. "Never again. I'm going to get you out of there. I swear to god, I am."

And I know exactly how to do it. No matter how much I hate what I'll have to do.

With my lips pressed into a tight line, I pull the little frame off the wall and slide the photo out. Tucking the lightly faded picture into my jacket's inner pocket, I turn on my heel and leave the room.

Stay the fuck alive, Nathan. Just stay alive. I'm coming.

CHAPTER THREE

My first impulse is to go straight to the auction house, but as it turns out, I don't exactly own anything suited to auctioning myself off.

Shocking, right?

Besides, Nathan's already too deep in with the vamps for this to be any kind of smash and grab job. If I'm going to properly infiltrate their hive, I need to do it the right way. And that means taking enough time to do it right.

So after finding another cab to take me home, I spend the rest of the night on the dark web, browsing the vampire fan chatrooms. Several hours in, I know exactly what I need to do to maximize my chances of being chosen as a blood tribute—everything from the dress to the scent. Eventually, I try to sleep a little, but it's largely useless. My eyelids don't want to stay closed, and I'm restless and twitchy all night.

After a few hours of sort-of-sleep, I haul myself out of bed and mainline almost an entire pot of coffee. Then I head out, hitting up several boutiques downtown to search for the perfect dress.

I know it as soon as I see it. I don't even bother trying it on, just hand my credit card to the woman behind the counter and try not to think about the number on the price tag.

Whatever it costs, whatever it takes, I'll fucking do it. I'm not letting my brother rot in a vampire palace.

When I get home, I hang the dress from the curtain rod over my living room window. The dark red fabric is the most colorful thing in my whole apartment—which isn't saying much, I guess. I didn't exactly put a whole lot of thought into decorating this place.

The walls are light gray, the carpet is dark gray, and the second-hand couch is a muted olive color. My bedroom is just as monochromatic, though the furniture is a little nicer. My captain's bed doubles as a weapons locker. So does the cedar chest at the foot of it. Nathan's old room is a gym now, but once I get him back here, I'll turn it back into a bedroom for him. I still have all his stuff stashed in a storage locker. Well, everything but the bongs, pipes, and syringes. I smashed the hell out of those.

Shoving my thoughts away from my struggles and failures as a sister, I gaze up at the dress again, sizing it up like I might do with a new weapon. Evaluating its usefulness for its intended purpose.

Then I pluck it down from the curtain rod and get to work, spending the next several hours making a few key alterations to the garment. Between modifying the dress and doing some additional research on the vamps' underground palace, the day flies by. It seems like all I do is blink, and suddenly, it's dark outside.

Time to get this show on the road.

Stripping out of my faded jeans and tee, I step into the dress and lace up the corset, then turn to look at myself in my bedroom mirror.

This gown is unlike anything I've ever had in my closet; it's brazen and eye-catching and absolutely gorgeous. The bodice is a corset, and the skirt flares out at the hip, with enough fabric for me to hide weapons inside it. Above the corset, my breasts are cupped in a semi-transparent halter which lets just enough of my nipples show to tease the eye. Below, the skirt and petticoats fall to my ankles, with a slit up to my hip on one side. I've sewn weapons between the layers of the skirt—just my two favorite knives, although I wish I could bring a whole fucking armory with me.

I do a practice spin in front of the mirror to make sure I've balanced it all properly and that the knives are truly undetectable. I think they are, but I can't be entirely sure since I can't really see how the back spins. I know I'll be dead if I'm caught smuggling weapons in there, but there's no way I'm leaving them at home.

I try to evaluate the odds in my head, but there are too many unknown variables. I know I look and smell good. I know that my weapons aren't strictly visible. I just don't know if I'm too obviously fit from fighting and training, or if any of them will recognize my face. I don't think I've ever left a witness after a kill, but there's really no way to be certain of that.

"Only one way to find out," I tell my reflection, grimacing slightly

Blowing out my cheeks, I slide my feet into the new stilettos I bought this morning. They're comfortable enough for what they are, but I can feel my anxiety start to increase as I straighten up. I can walk just fine, I'm light on my feet and have good balance. But there's no fucking way I could run or climb in these—not without breaking a leg or two.

That's the whole point, really. If I showed up in my black tactical gear and combat boots, they'd kill me before I could even get in the door. These shoes send a different kind of message.

And that message is: *prey on me, I can't get away if I change my mind.*

"I can't believe people actually do this shit for the thrill of it," I mutter. I may have a personal vendetta against vampires, but even if I didn't, I can't imagine myself voluntarily choosing to throw myself into their clutches as a blood tribute. As a fucking *groupie*.

Shaking off the impulse to check and double check my weapons, I lock my feet in with the thin straps on the shoes, tuck a bejeweled comb in my dark hair, slip a pair of blood-drop earrings in my ears, and turn around in front of the mirror again to look at the final result.

My sharp features look almost model-like when combined with the stunning getup and the makeup I applied before getting dressed. My blue eyes look even brighter next to the red of the earrings and the scarlet color of my lips.

Good enough.

Passable, anyway, assuming I can get rid of this scowl.

I try on a few bubble-headed smiles and settle on wide-eyed awe.

That'll work. Let's do this.

I throw on a ratty trench coat so I can get downtown without too much hassle. This dress would have me stopped for solicitation in a heartbeat. Not without cause, I suppose, considering what I'm about to go do.

The cab I hail only takes me three-quarters of the way there before I stop the driver and tell him to pull over. It's not so much because I'm afraid of being followed or traced, but because I really need to settle my nerves before I walk in there. Knowing that I'm going to be around dozens of vampires is making me itch to fight. I need to find *softness* somewhere inside of me, some sort of doe-eyed naivete, something to hold on to so that I can present the right face to these vermin.

The walk helps—a little, at least. Every time I feel my fingers curling into fists or my shoulders bunching up, I force myself to take a deep breath, hold it, and then release it.

When I finally arrive at my destination, I almost think I'm in the wrong place at first. The bar is fairly quiet, playing some soft-rock bullshit while middle-aged people sit around communing with their drinks. There's a subtle black door in the back beyond the bathrooms. The bartender catches my eye, glances down at my feet, and nods his head that way.

Perfect, thanks dude.

At least I look the part enough to fool the human bartender. It's not much, but it's a start, and I'll take it.

I follow his silent directions, heading toward the back. Through the door he indicated is a coat check, and beyond that, another door. The second door vibrates with the beat of the stage music beyond.

"Is there a cover charge to get into the club?" I ask the girl who's standing at a little lectern to one side of the door. My heart stills as I look into her crystal blue eyes. Her narrowing pupils tell me she's a vampire, and every instinct in me screams to take her out now, while no one is looking.

"Not for women," she drawls in a bored tone as she

takes my big coat and drapes it over one arm. "Here's your coat-check ticket. Have fun."

"Yeah, sure." I crumple the ticket in my palm and toss it to the floor as soon as I'm through the door. I'm not planning to come back for the jacket anyway.

The club is about what you'd expect. It's not at all my scene, but that doesn't matter. It's not why I'm here anyway. All I want is to find the door to the basement. Threading my way through the press of bodies, I pass by stages full of topless—and occasionally bottomless—women, keeping count of any vampires I notice. There are at least a dozen watching the dancers, and just as many dancing.

My stomach tightens, my jaw clenching. *I guess that's one way to get a meal.*

When I'm about halfway across the large space, a burly man steps in my path. I stop quickly enough not to run into him, and he eyes me for a second, his gaze running up and down my body.

"You look lost," he rumbles.

Shit. I knew I was being too obvious. I scramble to think of something to say, debating whether it's better to attack now before he has a chance to anticipate it—but then he leans down next to my ear and whispers, "Employment or tribute?"

"Tribute," I breathe.

He nods once and jerks his head, indicating for me to

follow him. I do, taking several more breaths to unclench my muscles again as he leads me to a curtain. When he draws it aside with one hand, I see stairs covered in red carpet leading down to the basement.

"Take a left at the bottom," he tells me. "Ask for Boris."

"Thanks."

Lifting the heavy skirts of my dress, I make my way down the stairs, not looking back at the man who waits at the top.

As I step off the last stair at the bottom, I can *feel* the change in the air. There's a thick atmosphere of sex and debauchery down here. A flat-screen TV is playing porn on mute, and neon arrows are pointing to the left. There's a window cut into the wall on the other side of the room with another bored-looking vampire sitting behind it. She flicks her gaze at me and away again, not seeming interested or impressed. She clearly knows why I'm here, and I allow that knowledge to bolster me a little. The disguise I picked is working.

Since the woman behind the window seems content to ignore me, I ignore her too, venturing deeper into the underground club. Scanning my surroundings with a subtle glance, I turn left and step through another curtain. This one leads to a narrow, dingy, poorly-lit hallway which, as soon as I turn the corner, becomes a narrow, dingy, poorly-lit tunnel.

My stomach churns. *Fucking hell.*

I wasn't hoping for puppies and rainbows, but this isn't what I was anticipating at all. It's creepy as shit, as if every level of this place I pass through is peeling back a layer on the vampires' veneer of humanity.

Down here, they clearly don't feel a need to keep up any pretenses.

But I grit my teeth and keep walking anyway. Not only do I refuse to back off and leave Nathan to his fate, but running would probably only make the vamps suspicious at this point, or give them an excuse to chase me down.

Never turn your back on a fucking predator. I learned that lesson a long time ago.

At the end of a tunnel, a huge man stands beside what can only be described as the biggest vault door I've ever seen. His arms are crossed, and he's got a gun on each hip. I don't know why a three-hundred-pound body building vampire needs any guns, but he's got them. He lowers his arms as I approach and looks me up and down. His eyes linger on the blood-drop earrings which are brushing seductively against my throat as I walk.

"Lost?" he asks gruffly.

Gotta be stupid. Gotta be vapid. Come on, breathy tone, wide eyes.

"I don't think so." I step closer to him and drop my voice to a stage whisper. Cue the drama. "I'm here to offer myself as tribute... to the vampires."

He frowns thoughtfully and circles me like a shark,

feeling me up with his eyes. I smell the hunger on his breath and see it in the bulge of his pants. I bite the tip of my tongue gently, just enough to remind myself to keep my expression neutral, but I hate the way he's looking at me. This expensive as fuck dress won't be worth a damn if he decides to take me for himself.

I stiffen my posture as his hand brushes my ass, my heart jolting into overdrive. I can't let him keep touching me, or he'll feel everything that I have hidden.

"This is the auction house, isn't it?" I ask, forcing my voice to sound uncertain and a little panicked. He drops his hand. "Did I come to the wrong place? A friend told me about it. I heard that... but maybe I was wrong..."

"Nah. This is it," he says. He looks me over once more then shrugs as if deciding I'm not worth the trouble. "You'll do, I guess."

He opens the door, and despite his casual dismissal of me, I can still feel his gaze glued to my neck. I suppress a shudder, reminding myself that this is why I'm here. I want this attention. I *want* to be noticed like that. At least for right now. Later, once I'm in the palace, I'll do whatever it takes to blend in to the damn wallpaper.

Shit. Do vampires even use wallpaper?

"Stupid question," I mutter to myself. "Not relevant, Mikka."

The auction house contrasts strikingly with the rough tunnel outside. The ceiling is so high that it fades away into the shadows as chandeliers plunge low over the crowd. Grand pillars and expensive chairs dot the marble floor. Every wall is a patchwork of intricately carved molding and ancient tapestries, with the occasional heavy oak door breaking up the pattern.

On the stage are twelve pedestals. People—humans—stand on eight of them.

A woman strikes a sensual pose, putting her neck on display. Another one stands stiffly, staring off unblinkingly at a shadowy part of the ceiling. I figure the first woman watches too many movies and the second one has too many gambling debts. I write them both off as idiots and do my damnedest to mimic the energy of the sultry woman.

A female vampire stands at the foot of the stage. I make a beeline toward her, and when she sees me coming, she holds out her hand to me with a smile.

"Welcome," she purrs. "Such a lovely tribute. Choose your pedestal, darling, and put on a show. It's a great honor to be chosen."

"I know," I breathe, pitching my voice a little higher and softer than usual. "Thank you so, so much."

Ugh. Fuck.

Suppress the shudder, Mikka.

I keep the awestruck expression firmly in place on my features all the way to the pedestal, subtly turning my head this way and that to get a closer look at the others as I walk. I'm surprised at how many tears I see on more than a few faces. It can't be *that* hard to avoid this place, can it? How are there so many people—men and women alike—who have ended up here against their will?

I shove the question out of my mind before the potential answers can make my blood boil. That path leads to exposure. I have to embody the fangirl, exude the fangirl, be one with the fangirl.

A particularly ugly vampire in the crowd catches my attention as I step onto my pedestal and smooth down my dress's heavy skirt. He's got a scarred, pock-marked face, but I force myself to wink at him and stroke my throat, shoving my disgust deep into the recesses of my mind.

Maybe I shove the disgust down a little *too* far, because when I cut my gaze away from the scar-faced vamp, the next man I look at actually looks attractive.

No, scratch that.

He looks fucking gorgeous.

He's standing by the door near the back of the crowd, watching everything play out before him. His broad shoulders and tan skin, thick brown hair, intense dark eyes make him look like the kind of vampire all the fangirls fantasize about—the kind with otherworldly beauty, the kind who can't possibly be human because no human could look that fucking sexy. A nose ring glitters on his face, and he's got his thick arms crossed over his chest, his features set into a stoic scowl.

I must stare at him for too long, taken aback by his

appearance, because he turns his head suddenly, catching my gaze. Our eyes meet, and his brows draw inward a little. His scowl softens.

My heart does a strange thud-thud in my chest, as if it tried to fit in an extra beat out of nowhere.

What the hell?

Adrenaline surges through me, panic not far after it, and it takes all my self-control not to react with a physical jerk.

Keep it together, Mikka. Maintain eye contact, maintain goopy expression, and analyze.

There are plenty of possible reasons for my strange reaction to this man.

I'm in a dangerous place surrounded by vampires with no way out, for one thing. That's extremely fucking stressful. I've been doing nothing but fight and hunt for the last month... maybe two.

When was the last time I even got laid?

I can't remember, and that's a bad thing. I learned a long time ago that the best way to keep a clear head and manage the stress that comes with this job is to have sex at least twice a month, preferably more. But I've been too busy hunting bloodsuckers recently to be in the mood to hunt down a good lay.

And the man standing by the wall is objectively attractive. He was human, once upon a probably very long time ago. And *if* he were still human, he's the kind of guy who would be very much my type.

That's all it is. Simple physical attraction.

Now that I'm sure I'm not being subtly seduced by this surreal environment or some kind of vampire pheromone or something, I relax into my role a little bit more. I flirt with the vampires nearest to me and show off my neck, letting my earrings caress my skin as I tilt my head. The moves are familiar and come easily to me. It's not the first time I've teased a vampire, although it *is* the first time I've done it without the intention of immediately killing the damned thing.

After a few moments, a vampire in a sleek, deep red tux jumps gracefully onto the stage with a microphone in his hand.

"Good evening, everyone," he purrs. "We have a lovely selection for you tonight. A stunning array of tributes just dying to be chosen."

His word choice sends a ripple of chuckles through the crowd. Gross. With his microphone still held loosely in his hand, he turns and scans the stage behind him. To my horror, his eyes land on me immediately. A grin spreads across his face, and he walks over, stalking toward me like the predator he is.

"Hello, my succulent little friend. Let's tell our audience about you, shall we? What's your name?"

"Darcy," I say, putting a flirty lilt into my voice. There's no fucking way I'm telling him my real name. I knew a girl in high school named Darcy, and I never really liked her. I think she ended up working as a stripper at a club on the outskirts of Baltimore, actually.

"Darcy." He rolls the word around on his tongue like he's tasting it, and goose bumps prickle over my skin. "That's a lovely name. Tell me, Darcy, what's your favorite food?"

Refusing to think too hard about how a lot of the occupants of this room would answer that question, I pretend to consider my answer.

"Well, I love fruit," I say with a little purr. "And red wine."

"Fruit and wine. We have ourselves a fine dessert here, gentlemen." He turns to grin at the crowd as if they're sharing an inside joke, then refocuses his attention on me. "You have a lovely physique, if you don't mind me saying so. How do you stay so fit and trim, Darcy?"

"Gymnastics." I give what I hope is a mysterious, sultry smile, drawing in a deep enough breath to make my breasts strain a little against the semi-transparent fabric of my top. "And I dance a lot."

"A dancer and a gymnast." His eyebrows rise a little, and now he's looking at me with *real* interest, not just the type meant to hype up the crowd. That's a good thing, but it still makes my skin crawl. "My, my, my, you're two dessert courses in one," he purrs. "Tell us a bit about why you're here, little one. Why do you want to become a blood tribute?"

Even though I've been expecting the question and have prepared a lie in advance, my jaw momentarily locks up, refusing to let me answer. I bite my lip, dragging it through my teeth and hoping that will be enough to cover up my internal struggle. Then I arch my back just a bit more, give him a sultry look up and down, and let my anger flutter like excitement in my pulse.

"I've dreamed of being a consort to a vampire for years," I say breathlessly. "You're all so strong and powerful. My greatest wish and desire is to be penetrated by your magnificent fangs and give myself to you. Any of you... *all* of you... I'm strong enough to take it."

A few murmurs and appreciative whistles break out in the crowd, turning my stomach. They're clearly buying it, which was the point. So why do I hate myself so much right now? I feel dirty, and the excited nods of agreement from a few of the girls onstage is making it so much worse. The fact that anyone honestly feels that way disturbs me.

The vampire in the red tux gives me one last slow perusal with his gaze, as if he's considering claiming me for himself. Then affixes the dazzling, charming smile to his face again and turns to address the crowd.

"Well, there you have it, ladies and gents. Darcy, the most willing little morsel you'll ever trifle with." He steps toward the woman on my right, sweeping an arm out in a gesture that encompasses her full form. "Next, a very curvaceous blonde beauty. What's your name, girl?"

She opens her mouth to answer his question, but I tune out the words, everything disappearing under the rush of blood in my ears.

I did it. I kept up the charade and managed to keep from blurting something I shouldn't.

Now I just have to hope I'm chosen.

CHAPTER FOUR

My heart doesn't stop racing as the auctioneer makes the rounds to the rest of the human women stationed on pedestals around me. Some of them gush and flirt with him, some seem too awed to do more than stare, and one or two are crying too hard to really answer any of his questions. Not that it matters. Their obvious fear and discomfort is in no way disqualifying—in fact, it's probably considered a plus for some of the vamps in this room.

Once all of the women have been introduced, bids are placed. Since every single vampire here belongs to the Vampire Clan of Baltimore, they're not bidding on us individually. Any women who are chosen will be considered tributes to the entire clan, brought to live in the palace for the duration of their contracted term.

I don't know much about how it works beyond that. Every bit of knowledge I have about the process for humans to sell themselves to vampires is from snippets and rumors I've picked up on the street, stories about someone who's friend of a friend traded their freedom and blood for a time in exchange for money.

I have no idea who makes the ultimate decision about how much to bid or who to bid on, but when the auctioneer starts the bidding, several serious looking vampires step forward. They're much less raucous than the rest of the crowd, probably representatives from the palace, and they point to the women they want and call out numbers as the man in the red suit keeps everything running smoothly.

The first time one of the vamps points at me, my heart leaps. I'm tempted to just accept his offer right away, but I worry about looking too eager and drawing suspicion. Even vampire fangirls probably do it partly for the money, so I hold out until I get a higher offer and then nod to the auctioneer.

The whole thing only takes a few minutes. Once the bidding ends, the girls who weren't chosen step down from their pedestals, some of them looking relieved and others disappointed. The woman who greeted me when I first walked in ushers them off the stage, and they disappear through the crowd. I lose track of them before they reach the door, dragging my attention back to what's going on around me.

"Lovely, lovely. Another successful auction. Now I know you're all ready for a feast, am I right?"

As he speaks, the auctioneer moves to the center of the stage while a red-tinged spotlight follows him. The crowd whoops enthusiastically, as if they don't do this all the damn time. He drinks in their excitement like it's lifeblood —ironically—and continues to amp them up. As he's gesticulating, he moves back behind the pedestals, to the center of the stage. He pulls a rope that I mistakenly assumed was a pull rope for the velvet curtain, and a second later, the whole stage begins rocking and shaking under my feet.

"Escorts, to your tributes," the auctioneer says.

Just like that, there's a massive vampire by my side. His chest is bare except for the two straps of leather crossing it, which end in a belt slung low around his hips. He's wearing combat boots, and his pants are covered in chains. Apocalypse punk seems to be the standard uniform for these "escorts," though none of them are wearing exactly the same thing. He glances down at me, clearly bored. He must have wanted a flight risk. He keeps glancing eagerly at the tear-streaked woman in front of us, silently daring her to bolt.

She doesn't. She seems smarter than that, even if she did end up on the auction block along with the rest of us. She must've done something stupid at some point to get here.

The part of the stage behind the pedestals has sunk into the ground now, revealing a broad hidden passage almost as big as the auction room itself. At the end, stairs lead down into the dark. I glance around for a mechanism to open the stage from below, but I can't see anything. I want to look harder, but I don't think I can get away with it. Not now.

Two vampires guard the top of the stairs. The escort-tribute pair in front of me is stopped, the tribute is searched, and then they're allowed to pass.

I deliberately keep my breathing even and steady, trying to keep my heart rate down. I expected to be searched and prepared for that eventuality, but there's always a chance I didn't do as well as I think I did. I'm not a master-level seamstress, although I'm usually handy enough when I need to be.

Unaware of my inner anxiety, my escort drags me to a halt in front of security. I paste on my most inviting smile and look up at the guards through my lashes.

"Is it a... strip search?" I ask, trying to look both nervous and excited by the idea, instead of just nauseated.

"No," one of them says shortly. His expression is hard and blank. Unlike the raucous crowd who came to watch the auction, he's clearly just here to do his job. "Only a quick once-over. Don't need you accidentally bringing garlic down there."

I gasp, forcing my eyes to go wide. "Garlic? I would never do that. It could hurt someone."

Not even bothering to acknowledge my words, the guard jerks his chin, and his friend gives me a perfunctory pat-down. My nerves scream with awareness as he reaches for the skirt of my dress, but he doesn't run his hands over the length of the fabric, just parts the slit at one side and reaches beneath the heavy layers to check that I don't have anything strapped to my legs.

My breath hitches a little, but I hope he'll think that's just from having his hands on me. It's a good fucking thing I hid my weapons, but I'm so used to having daggers sheathed at my thighs when I hunt that I almost worry he'll somehow feel the lingering imprint of metal against my skin.

But he doesn't. After running his hands up my thighs again, *way* too close to my fucking vagina for comfort, he steps back, then nods and waves us through.

"Pretty little thing, that one," I hear him murmur to his stoic counterpart as we walk away. "More muscular than I usually like them, but soft where it counts."

I almost manage to suppress a shudder. My escort glances down at me, a vague sort of concern on his face.

"The stairs are cold," he says, his voice deep and gravelly. "Palace is warm, though. Don't worry."

"I can't wait to get there," I say breathlessly, rubbing my arms as if for warmth. I'm not even cold—I've worked in ice storms with just enough layers on to avoid frostbite—but I'd rather him assume that than realize that I'm disgusted by this whole thing.

The stairs are loud. They're steel on steel, with rattling grates on every step. The walls are smooth, hard, and multi-faceted in just the right way to make every sound echo. The railings aren't really railings, but smooth steel bars standing vertically from floor to ceiling, with a handspan between each one.

Fuck. So much for sneaking out once I find Nathan. The stairs are clearly set up to be an early warning system of any intruders—or escapees—and there's no chance of climbing a bannister.

We go three stories down beneath the ground. I don't see any other openings, just smooth walls at every landing. There are more guards at the bottom, but they don't stop us. We're waved through to a steel vault door, which opens from the inside after one of the escorts nods his head to a camera embedded in the wall. I try to suppress the curling dread in my stomach as I'm herded forward with the rest of the women. So far, I'm not seeing any easy way out. I can't imagine that this is the only entrance to the palace, not with how big the place must be. There have to be other ways in and out. Hopefully they won't be quite as secure.

The vault door closes with a dull thud behind us, and I glance around my new surroundings to see a female vampire waiting just inside. She steps forward, giving us a smile that doesn't quite reach her eyes. Her face makes her look middle-aged, but that just means that's how old she was when she turned—it has no relation to the actual amount of time she's walked the earth.

"Welcome, darlings," she coos, pressing her hand to a few girls' cheeks. "Oh, so many pretty things. We leave the men here. Follow me."

Once again, we're all herded forward, and I get the unpleasant sensation that I'm part of a flock of sheep being led to the slaughter.

This place is a maze. I'm trying to keep track of all the twists and turns, flights up and down, long hallways and random doors, but I can't honestly be sure I'll know how to get back to that entrance even if I do figure out a way to get up the stairs without dying.

The vampire matron moves at a vampire pace, which is just slightly faster than comfortable for the average human. It doesn't bother me, but I need it to look and sound like it does. I put on a show, moving at the same rate as the two girls nearest me. Jog for a bit. Get a little winded. Fall back, catch up.

The first thing she does is bring us to a large room that looks sort of like a massive study or a library. There are contracts laid out on the cherry wood table in the middle of the room, and she leads us over to them.

"You'll just need to sign these, my dears."

I step forward, willing my hand not to shake as I reach

for the elaborate ink pen next to my contract. These fuckers could get simple ball point pens if they wanted. They're living in the twenty-first century along with the rest of us, but they clearly like to go for the effect of making us sign with these ancient and intimidating looking things.

The contract is long and full of a million lines of fine print. I see a few girls try to scan theirs quickly, glancing at the matron as if expecting to have their heads bitten off by her for dawdling, but most of them just pick up the pens and scrawl their names.

I do the same, only pausing long enough to check that the bid amount is accurate. Honestly, the words of the contract don't matter to me. I don't plan on staying for the full term of the contract anyway, and if the vamps find out why I'm really here, they'll kill me in a heartbeat, contract or no.

Another little piece of my soul seems to shrivel up and die as I scrawl *Darcy Claymore* at the bottom of the page. Even though the signature doesn't say Mikka Dawson, the act of signing a blood tribute contract still gives me the fucking creeps.

Once everybody's finished with their contracts, two silent vampires come to collect them, and the female vamp ushers us out of the library.

She leads us down a few more long hallways before we finally reach the wing of the palace where the blood tributes are kept. We're each deposited in our own rooms with a promise that the matron will come back to collect us again soon and instructions to get changed into something "suitable."

With that alarming pronouncement, the female vampire disappears.

I close my door, thanking whatever gods might be listening for small favors. I expected to be bunking with other tributes, or at the very least, sharing a room. Keeping my façade up interminably would have exhausted me, probably to the point of making a mistake. I can never afford mistakes, but especially not now.

After waiting a few moments to make sure that no one is going to burst in, I strip out of my dress and stretch. Being out of that constricting thing makes me feel like myself again, and I revel in it—especially since I know the feeling isn't going to last.

Kicking off my shoes, I work out the kinks in my toes and the arches of my feet, still stretching out my back and shoulders too. My muscles are used to all kinds of punishment, but stiletto heels and corsets are pure torture. I know I don't have a lot of time before the matron will return, but it feels so good to be in my own skin that I push the limits a little bit. They can't very well bring me to a feast naked, after all.

Well... maybe they can.

I shudder at that thought and decide I'd better get dressed quick and not risk it. After glancing around quickly, I move toward the old-fashioned wardrobe in one corner of the room and fling it open.

It's full of clothes in my size, and my brows knit as I pull a few items out to examine them. What the hell? How did they do this? There must've been some kind of communication between the auction master and the vampires who work in the palace. Once the tributes were on their way down, they probably started preparing our rooms for us, based on information provided by the auctioneer.

The clothes are all tight, revealing, and verging on gaudy. Frosting for the dessert, I guess. Useless and eye-catching.

I grimace, rifling through several outfits quickly. There has to be something in here which will let me disappear into the crowd.

The most conservative thing in the entire wardrobe is a long, black, form-fitting dress with transparent lace cut-outs all over it. It'll have to do. I wriggle into it and make a face at myself in the full-length mirror set along one wall. The fucking thing is so low cut that my cleavage is on *full* display. The vee dips down to my belly button, and the sleeves are three-quarter length, leaving my neck and wrists on display. The lace cut-outs are strategically placed to give peek-a-boo shots of my legs and the underside of my ass.

For fuck's sake.

At least it isn't pink.

Once I'm dressed, I quickly gather up my discarded gown from the floor, scanning the room again. There aren't a lot of hiding places in here, but I find an empty drawer in the bottom of the wardrobe. After messing with it for a minute, I manage to pull the bottom out of it. There's enough space beneath for me to rig a false bottom, but it'll take time. It'll take time to get my weapons out of my dress, too, unless I decide to just tear the stupid thing to shreds. But that seems too risky.

Too many people saw me in it. What if one of the vamps who came to watch the auction tells me to wear it later?

On the other hand, I can't risk having someone come in here and try to grab my dress to wash it while I'm gone. The weapons were hidden well enough to avoid detection so far, but if this thing gets put in the laundry, it'll be all over.

There's only one thing to do. I put the bottom back in the drawer and fold my dress up tight, wadding it into as small of a bundle as possible. Then I shove it in the drawer, wincing as the heavy weapons thump dully against the wooden bottom.

There. I'll deal with it later, after the sun comes up and the vampires go to bed.

I choose a pair of strappy black shoes from the wardrobe. They fit perfectly, which stresses me out more than the clothes do. A trained eye can glean a person's waist size pretty easily, but shoe size? That's psychic-level insight. If these vampires have a psychic working for them, I'm screwed. But unlike my towering stilettos, these shoes only have the smallest hint of a heel, and they lace up in all the right spots. I could run in these if I had to, which is always a plus.

I'm about to take my jewelry off when someone knocks on my door. "Are you decent, my dear?"

I smirk in spite of myself. *Not usually.*

"Yes, come in."

The matron who escorted us through the halls earlier opens the door. She smiles when she sees me, although once again, nothing in her eyes seems to change to reflect the curve of her lips.

"We didn't formally meet earlier. I'm Anastasyia," she says, holding out her hand. "Come on out here. Now that everyone's dressed, I'll show all of you around."

I join the other girls in the hall outside. The one who was crying the hardest on the way down here isn't weeping anymore. She just looks tired and resigned now.

"I don't know how much you were told already," Anastasyia says. "I always tell the men to leave the orientation to me, but some of them can't help themselves and start talking on the way down the stairs." She waves her hands in a fluttering gesture as if to brush that aside. "Anyway, this is the female tribute wing. All the women live here. No males allowed. Men live on the other side, where female tributes are forbidden. The vampires don't like their humans mixing—pregnant tributes cause all kinds of moral and social complications, as you can imagine. It never ends well."

The way she talks about it makes me certain that it's happened before, probably more than just once. Rage simmers at the base of my spine, and I clench my toes inside my shoes to keep from clenching my fists.

"If you'll follow me, I'll show you around." Anastasyia gestures to the doors that dot the hallway around us. "These are, obviously, your bedrooms. You have one bathroom for every four bedrooms. Be respectful, and keep your space clean. I usually don't have too much trouble with new tributes, but keep in mind that the binding ceremony won't be for a few weeks."

"Will we still live in this wing after the binding ceremony?" one girl asks.

"If you aren't chosen by a particular vampire, then yes, you'll stay here. If you *are* chosen, you'll stay wherever your bonded vampire decides you should stay. Most of them prefer to have their bound tributes live with them in their rooms. A comfortable arrangement, I'm told, if occasionally exhausting."

Some of the girls giggle at that, sharing secretive glances or nudging each other. It's all I can do to keep from shaking my head in disappointment.

She's not talking about sex, you idiots.

She's talking about the exhaustion that comes from losing a portion of blood every single day for the rest of your short life.

This is why I didn't bother to read the full contract before I signed it. Because I know that, no matter how much they try to disguise it in flowery language, this bargain is set up to benefit the vamps at the expense of humans. Ostensibly, we're all here for an agreed upon period of time in exchange for an agreed upon amount of money. But if any vampires decide they want to keep one of us forever, they can do that, and there won't be shit we can do about it.

Or at least, that's how it's meant to work. I have no intention of letting any vampire get their fangs that deep in me.

The vampire matron leads us further down the hallway, turning left before gesturing to a large room visible through a wide, arched doorway.

"Here is the common room, where you can watch TV, play boardgames, read—we have all kinds of things for you to do on your down time. You will have computer access, but you should know that everything is strictly monitored, so don't go posting on Read It or whatever it's called about how you're a blood tribute. Social media is strictly prohibited."

There aren't as many disappointed noises as I

expected. Up until now, I was pretty sure that most of these women did this for the bragging rights among their fellow vampire fanatics, but I guess not.

"And around this corner is—oops!"

Anastasyia begins to lead us down another corridor, but as we make the turn, we run right into a man coming from the opposite direction.

Well, *she* sidesteps him. I run into him.

I'm usually much lighter on my feet, but the pressure of the long evening, combined with the suddenness of his approach, catch me off-guard. I slam into his broad chest, and he grabs my arms to keep me upright.

As I steady myself and glance up, I find myself staring at a guy who looks to be about my age or a little older, maybe twenty-five or twenty-six, with wavy blonde hair and eyes that remind me of a sunset through a chunk of amber. They almost look golden, and they're framed by thick lashes that only accentuate their startling color more.

"Oops, sorry," he murmurs, his voice friendly and amused. "You okay there?"

He rubs my arms as the group of women behind me grinds to a halt, sending pleasant sensations sparking across my skin. His gentle hands and unabashed smile make him the kind of guy I'd want to pick up after a brutal day in the field, just to bask in his optimism for a while.

"Yeah." I shake my head, grinning a little in spite of my dire circumstance. "Fine."

Releasing my arms, he steps back a little and looks over my shoulder to address the rest of the group. "So sorry, ladies. I seem to have stumbled into the wrong wing. I'll get the hang of this place eventually. I'm Connor, by the way."

His eyes twinkle in a way that lights up his whole face as he speaks. Damn, he really is cute as fuck. It's a shame that fraternizing with the opposite gender isn't allowed around here. I have a sudden wild thought that maybe I can smuggle him aboveground with me when I break Nathan out of here. No one this full of sunshine deserves to be locked up several stories below ground as food for vampires.

"How long have you been here?" the girl behind me asks breathlessly.

"Ah, just a few months. You'd think that would be long enough to learn your new home, but..." He shrugs haplessly, running a hand through his messy blond hair. "The other vampires keep promising me that I'll get the hang of it, but I think they sorely underestimate my ability to screw things up."

He chuckles. The sound is warm and deep, but my brain is too busy short-circuiting to appreciate it.

The other *vampires*?

This guy is a bloodsucker?

"But it's great fun," he continues, breaking out into another wide smile that displays even white teeth—and four pointed fangs. "Trying to figure out immortality and social rules and stuff all over again, while also mapping out a castle the size of my last neighborhood? Man, they just tossed me in here like, sure, you can swim!"

The women behind me are laughing at his jokes, and I give a feeble attempt at a giggle to try to blend in. But I'm still trying to wrap my head around this new piece of information.

He's a newly turned vampire. Maybe that accounts for his sweet vibe and upbeat attitude—but I don't know, I've met vampires who had only been turned recently who were already bloodthirsty psychos. Maybe he is too, when he isn't showing off for a bunch of tributes.

Why is he even bothering, anyway? Doesn't he have all the power here? Why make the effort to charm us when he could just order us to do whatever he wants?

Connor steps to one side, sweeping his arm out in an over-the-top chivalrous gesture to indicate that we could proceed. "I'll get out of your way. You ladies look like you have places to be." He shoots the matron a look, wrinkling his nose. "Um, Anastasyia?"

"You're looking for the main staircase again?"

He nods sheepishly.

She sighs. "Keep going this way, turn right at the end of the hall, take your first left, and it'll be right there."

"Thanks. This is the last time I'll ask, I promise. Well, maybe second to last."

He grins at her, and for the first time, I see her smile

reflected in her eyes as she nods at him. As he heads away, she turns back to us.

"Come on girls, you have more to see." She starts walking down the corridor again, and the group falls in behind her. "Now, most of the time you'll be having dinner with the vampires in the great hall, but for breakfast and lunch, you'll be on your own. Up ahead is the kitchen for this wing. Same rules as the bathroom, respect each other and clean up after yourselves. I don't want to have to ground anybody from—"

I stop listening, dragging my feet a little and glancing back over my shoulder. Connor is heading away down the hall, but he looks over his shoulder at the same moment I do, and our eyes meet. His brow furrows thoughtfully, some expression passing across his face that I'm too far away to read.

I can't believe he's a fucking vampire.

When we first crashed into each other, I got a good vibe from him. I *liked* him—liked his goofy smile and relaxed demeanor.

How the hell did that happen? Have my instincts already been blunted that badly by this role I'm playing?

Is there a chance I've met him before, out on the streets somewhere? Have we ever faced off in a dark alley? No, I don't think so. I would have remembered those eyes, that posture. Besides, I can't really picture Connor hunting in the streets. He seems too... nice for that.

I snap my head forward, gritting my teeth. I'm not going to stand here and rationalize vampires. They're all inherently monsters, and no amber eyes or brilliant smile can change that fact.

Get your head on straight, Mikka. Face forward, don't look back. Vampires aren't nice. They thrive on hunger, rage, lust, and pride. That's it. Don't humanize them, or you'll never get out of this fucking place alive.

CHAPTER FIVE

STEELING MY SPINE, I pick up my pace to rejoin the others, since I've fallen behind the group.

The crying girl is trailing behind the pack too. The tear tracks on her face have dried, but she still looks sad as hell. She doesn't seem interested in the library or kitchen or anything else. She cringes each time we pass an oil-painted portrait of a vampire and keeps shifting her arms to cover her cleavage and hips, tugging her skirt this way and that to give maximum coverage.

She clearly doesn't want to be here, playing this role she's been forced into. That was obvious from the beginning, but now...

I've never been big on alliances. I work alone. Teaming up with someone else or creating some kind of partnership has always seemed to be more trouble than it would be worth. But in a situation like this, making a similarly-minded friend might be helpful.

"Hey," I murmur to her in a low voice. "You doing okay?"

She glances mournfully at me and shrugs. "As okay as I'm ever going to be again, I guess."

"Yeah. Can't really argue with that."

She looks startled by my blunt, quiet words, then narrows her eyes at me. "Really? Seems like you wanted to be here just as bad as anybody."

"Seems like you don't," I shoot back, dodging the question. "So why *are* you?"

She looks like she's going to cry again. *Please don't, please don't.* She takes a breath to stop the tears, and I let out a quiet breath of relief. I'm not good with tears.

"It's my mom," she tells me in a voice barely louder than a whisper. "She's sick. She's always been sick, and she's going to keep being sick for the rest of her life. Last year, her Parkinson's got worse. Way worse. She can barely see anymore, and her flare-ups never end so she can hardly move. Her medicine alone costs so much I had to take three jobs just to pay for it, and I couldn't make enough to pay for a caretaker for her. She fell last month."

"Oh, no."

The girl nods and bites her trembling lip. "I wasn't there. She was alone on the floor for ten hours, and I wasn't there. She didn't break anything, but the bruises and the shock to her system made her symptoms so bad she couldn't get out of bed for days. I needed a nurse for her."

Fuck. That's awful. But there had to be some other solution than *this*. I open my mouth to say something, but before I can get a word out, the dark-haired girl raises a hand to cut me off.

"I know, I know, there are programs in place to help with things like that, and I've been looking into those for months and months already. I had my mom on a bunch of waiting lists and things. I called my brother for help, but he loves money more than anything else and isn't going to 'waste' his on her. He's a dick, honestly. But it gets worse."

"I can't imagine how, but go on."

She almost smiles at that, her hazel eyes glassy with unshed tears. "The cost of her medicine went up. So did rent, at the same time. I was already working three jobs and barely had enough money to scrape by before that happened. I sold everything I ever owned that had any kind of value, except the things my mom needs to be comfortable. We were about to get evicted. I begged my landlord for more time—I even offered to sleep with him if he could cut us a break. He took the offer and then denied any memory of a deal, so even after all that, I was still going to get evicted."

I narrow my eyes, my jaw clenching. Vampires aren't the only monsters in this godforsaken city. "What a fucking prick."

"Right? But the end of the month got closer and closer, and I needed like ten thousand dollars in my hand. I could only think of three ways to do it in that timeframe. Since I don't know how to hook a high-roller and I can't push drugs without talking the customer out of the sale, that left vampires."

"You didn't sell yourself for ten thousand, did you?" I ask, barely managing to keep my voice to a low hiss as I drop my head a little, catching her gaze.

That's not nearly enough. Her mom'll be in the same position next month, and this girl will still be down here.

She shakes her head. "No. I sold myself for my mom's health, well-being, and financial security until the day of her natural death, plus funeral costs. I couldn't put a number on that and neither could the vampires, not with how unstable the economy is. So the deal is a fluid one. She'll have four nurses who rotate shifts, so she'll never be alone. She'll have food and medicine and drivers to take her to and from her appointments. She'll have rent and utilities covered, along with anything else she could possibly want or need."

"That seems like a generous offer," I say slowly. "How do you know they'll hold up their end?"

She smiles sadly. "I don't. That's why, when I negotiated all of this before the auction, I insisted on monthly updates. I'm allowed to talk on the phone with her whenever I want, as long as I don't tell her what I'm really doing. If I'm good, and if I bond with a vampire who allows it, I might even get to visit her someday."

I squeeze her hand clumsily, trying to comfort her even as fury boils inside me. She hasn't done anything wrong. She's been forced into this, just like Nathan was, but she's even more innocent than he is. She's done everything right, trying to help her mom and keep a fucking roof over their heads. How could she have ended up here? The whole fucking system is rigged.

"I had no idea," I mutter. "I'm sorry."

She breathes deeply, clearly trying to pull herself together and put on a brave face. "It's okay. Mom's taken care of, and that's what matters. I did it, and I did it without resorting to crime. Which I would have done, if I'd known how to profit off of it, but I'm just not good at breaking rules."

No, it's not fucking okay. None of this is goddamn okay.

I turn my head away before I go off on a tangent that will give me away if Anastasyia overhears. I need a distraction or something. My heart is beating way too fast.

As if in response to my silent prayer, the vampire matron claps her hands together, drawing my attention.

"Okay, girls! Straighten up, get smiles on those faces, and clear your minds. It's dinner time."

As she speaks, she pushes a wide set of doors open, revealing a massive banquet hall. Chandeliers drip from the ceiling, scattering light to reflect off the excessive amount of crystal glassware on the tables. Blood red roses cluster in centerpieces and wreaths, with petals scattered around like this is some kind of boudoir photo shoot. Pink and red satin chairs reflect their colors on the gold-vein marble floor, set close to ornate tables topped with delicate black cloth.

The tables are all arranged around a huge dance floor which spirals off to kiss the edge of a raised stage, where musicians are busily setting up classical instruments. I can't tell if they're human or vampire from this distance. I'm not sure it matters. To my left is a long, formal-looking table on a slightly raised platform. All the chairs at that table are set up on one side of it, so whoever sits there will get an uninterrupted view of the whole hall. The chair in the center looks like a throne. The rest of them are red velvet.

There's gold clinging to things wherever I look.

It's opulent. It's extravagant. It's a disgusting pit of animal violence dressed up to look civilized. More than civilized. Elite.

Jesus fucking Christ. It's getting harder and harder to keep my fury in check. I hate every bit of this palace, but I think this dining hall just became my least favorite room in the whole place. Honestly, I almost would've rathered a bare room with filth on the floor and bloodstains on the wall. At least that would've been an accurate reflection of what this place is.

Anastasyia leads us to a table—it's right in the middle, out in the open, practically an invitation for attack—and tells us to sit. Then she positions herself at the head of our table and gives us all a once-over, her expression serious.

"Okay, girls, before the vampires get here, I need to give you a few reminders. First, any vampire is permitted to drink from you, for now. The bonding ceremony is in three weeks, and the rules change after that. If nobody chooses to bond with you, you will remain general tributes until either your contract expires or you die, whichever comes first."

I want to ask her how many people are actually allowed to finish out their contracts, but I don't think I could phrase it the right way. I'm aching to blow my own cover and rally the tributes to storm the castle, but I know better. More than half of these girls are listening raptly, their eyes full of stars and their hearts beating fast. They're into this. Really into it.

"The best thing I can tell you is to relax. It's going to hurt the first time. Just like everything else, right?" She gives a wry smile, as if we're all girlfriends dishing over cocktails. "But you'll get used to it. I'll be at that table by the wall if any of you need me, but... try not to need me. Honestly, you'll do better in the long run if you navigate on your own from the start. They sometimes like to pit tributes against one another. Don't buy into it, it'll just cause trouble for you. I—" She breaks off, glancing toward the high table. "Oh! Time to go. Good luck, girls!"

She strides gracefully away to join two other women at a table by the wall. I wonder if they're other matrons in charge of keeping an eye on the female "stock."

The tables around us start to fill up with women, other blood tributes who've been here longer than we have. They all have their hair pulled up away from their necks. I expect to see scars and holes on the more experienced tributes' throats, but there aren't any—at least, none I can pick up from this distance. If the scars are there, they're small.

The entire room is filling up fast now, with humans and vampires alike, but I have yet to see any male tributes. I'm almost relieved. I don't know yet how I'm going to get a message to Nathan without setting off all kinds of alarms, and I could really use a night to solve that problem.

My attention is everywhere as sounds and activity fill the large hall. I force myself to look around slowly, in no particular kind of pattern, rather than flick my eyes all over searching for weak spots. It's harder than I thought it would be, but I keep taking deep, slow breaths, letting my tension gather in spots where it won't be noticeable as I keep my face relaxed.

I can feel the vampires in the room, feel their gazes on me, their hunger and debauchery. I'm crouched behind enemy lines, and I've got to look like I enjoy the experience.

As I continue to subtly scan the room, my gaze drifts toward the high table—and my heart almost stops.

He's attacking her.

The dark-haired vampire sitting on the throne is clutching a scantily-clad woman in a hungry embrace, his mouth buried in her neck.

My stomach twists. Every fiber of my being itches to take him down right here and now so I can save that poor girl. But then she moans. I snap my attention to her face. Her mouth is open, red and full, her brow creased, her arms twisting to grip the chair. She's writhing, yes... but not to escape.

Holy fucking shit, she's about to come.

My twisted stomach flips in a weird way, a *new* way, pouring lava down my insides, melting me to my core. I don't even recognize the feeling at first. I don't get aroused like this, not unless I'm super drunk and kneeling in front of washboard abs. Even then, it's not intense like this. Sex is a tool. Like stilettos or whiskey or a really good blade. My job demands regular, efficient release. Sex with a stranger is the best way to get it.

But sex with a stranger has never, ever made me feel like this.

I can't look away. I'm disgusted, *horrified*, but that doesn't seem to make any difference to my fucking body.

She's in ecstasy. How is that possible?

I've seen vampires feed more times than I can count. It's always brutal. Their victims beg if they can, cry out in agony if they can't, and are always left dead or traumatized. This girl doesn't look traumatized at all. She looks blissful, like there's nowhere else on earth she'd rather be.

I must stare for too long, or maybe I make a noise without realizing it. As if he's sensed my attention, the dark haired vampire opens his eyes. His gaze snaps to mine, pinning me in place with irises that are the exact shade of dark gray as storm clouds.

CHAPTER SIX

Fight.

Run.

Freeze.

The conflicting impulses to do all three of those things ricochet through me as my eyes lock with his.

God, I wish I had my weapons on me.

I'd be an idiot to use them in here, but just having the cold steel pressed against my thighs would make me feel better.

My heart's racing. Dammit. I need to breathe, need to slow it down, but the darkly handsome vampire at the head table is still watching me. He slides his fangs out of the woman's throat, and she squeaks a little moan, like he'd just pulled his dick out. He licks the blood off her neck and his tongue closes her wounds.

They can do that? Motherfucker. Those bastard street vamps never do that.

He gives her a sultry look and gently pushes her off his lap. She gazes back at him like she's in love, her chest rising and falling with deep breaths as she turns and wobbles happily away. But he's not watching her go. No, his gaze has settled on *me* again, and it feels like he's looking right through me.

A shiver trickles through me as he licks the last few drops of blood from his lips. He looks predatory. Possessive. Terrifying.

So why does he also look sexy?

"Oh god. Do you think she's his bonded?" The full-figured blonde girl beside me poses the question to no one in particular.

A sparkly-eyed redhead with a perfect build, perfect skin, and perfectly symmetrical face picks up a fork and toys with it, laughing softly as she eyes the blonde girl. "Fuck, no. Don't you keep your ears open at all? Prince Bastian doesn't keep bonded humans. He prefers to… sample the whole buffet, so to speak."

I frown. "That doesn't make sense. He's the prince, isn't he? He could have anyone he wanted, and as many of them as he wants."

The redhead purses her lips at me and flicks a handful of perfectly manicured fingernails dismissively. "You know how men are, don't you? He's a wild one, from what I hear.

Doesn't want to get tied down, doesn't want to be stuck with any one tribute for too long." She smiles sweetly at me, but I can see behind the mask well enough to know she might as well be baring her teeth. "I don't think I got your name, sweetheart. Who are you?"

"Darcy," I say flatly.

"Winona," she drawls, extending a hand.

I shake it briefly. I've got calluses on my calluses and enough strength built up to crush her dainty little bones. A flash of disgust crosses her face, but she tucks it quickly behind her perfectly friendly mask.

"And you?" she asks the blonde beside me.

"Chelsea," the blonde drawls, as if it doesn't matter anyway.

"My name's Jessica." The girl I spoke to in the hall pipes up. She sounds a little desperate for a friend.

Winona dismisses her with a cutting glance. "Nobody cares, sweets. You obviously don't want to be here. The vampires will sense that about you, and you'll get stuck in general tribute limbo forever. Just accept it."

Jessica's face twists like she's about to cry again. I clear my throat and lean forward, then remember I'm conversing with women and sit up straight instead. I'm used to dealing with monsters and men—there's a whole different set of body language rules for that.

"General tribute seems like a better role in the long

run," I say. "Being bonded to a vampire sounds kind of crappy."

Winona's eyes widen in shock. "What? Come on, be realistic. Would you really rather be common fodder for all the vampires, for any nobody to stick his fangs in whenever he wants to, to be passed around like some prostitute?"

I shrug. "Rather be a prostitute than a puppy."

Jessica looks at me curiously and Chelsea shifts uncomfortably in her chair. Winona's smile has turned to ice.

"A puppy," she repeats with a breathy, unconvincing laugh. "Is that what you call it? To be permanently bonded to a powerful vampire—someone like the prince, or even one of the lesser members of the court, would give you the power. Haven't you heard the saying, sweetheart? Behind every powerful man is a woman pulling his strings? You would be the string puller. As a general tribute, you're just *meat*."

I can't help but laugh at her. "You think you'd be the one pulling the strings? Jesus. Tell the truth, Winona. You've obviously done enough research to know the answer. What happens to a tribute once they're bonded to a vampire?"

She flushes a pretty pink, and her eyes narrow almost imperceptibly. "I think everybody at this table knows just as much about it as I do."

Several girls shake their heads. A couple just look away.

"Please tell me." A slight girl with wide green eyes glances back and forth between me and Winona. "One of you. Either of you. Tell me. I... I thought bonding was just like... a promise or something, that you'd be exclusive or whatever with one vampire until your contract expires."

A smile spreads across my face, and not a very nice one. I don't take my eyes off Winona as I speak. "You think anyone survives to see their contract expire? Really?"

"Oh shut up, both of you." A girl across the table tightens the wrap around her hair and drops her elbows on the table, regarding all of us with a steel-eyed gaze. "You want to know what happens when you're bonded to a vampire, *I'll* fuckin' tell you."

"Oh?" Winona says icily, her nose way up in the air. "And what do you know, homegirl?"

That mocking sneer she adds to the last word turns her beautiful face terribly ugly. I wonder if she knows it'll stick that way.

Homegirl blinks at her once, slowly, then turns back toward the green-eyed girl who's still watching this all play out with a terrified expression on her face.

"The blood bond is a ritual that ties you to a single vampire. It connects you to them. Once you're bonded, you never want to leave. You crave their presence. You're addicted to them. Addicted to feeding them. Y'all remember the first time you had good sex? Like really good, *good* sex. The kind you keep thinking about for days and days, the kind that makes you wet just remembering it? That's the feeling you'll get when your vampire touches you. You'll do whatever they say, go wherever they tell you, become whoever they want you to become, just so you'll never have to be without them."

She turned her cold gaze to me, her jaw set in a way I recognize. I think I've worn that exact expression before, in fact. "Some tributes *do* outlive their contracts. But bonded tributes will kill themselves before they'll leave. I've seen it."

Winona scoffs. "You've seen it, have you? You got here the same time we did. What are you, some baby psychic? Stop scaring the other girls."

"*You* outlived your contract," I murmur, meeting her steely gaze. "Your first contract."

"And my second," she shoots back, a note of pride in her voice. "This'll be my third, and I'll outlive this one too. You know why?"

"I'm more interested in how."

She smirks at me. "Because I'm too trashy for these classical fucks. They wanna taste the forbidden fruit, but they'll be damned if they'll be attached to it. I'm good at what I do. I take care of myself and I taste good. But I never ask for too high of a bid price each time, so I'm never here long enough for any of them to get stupid ideas into their heads."

I get that. "Okay," I say. "So, why?"

She shrugs. "I like money."

With that blunt answer, her expression closes along with her mouth.

Conversation over.

I like this chick. I wonder why she's *really* doing this, but I'm not going to push the issue. It's a distraction I don't need anymore, not now that the unsettling burn of arousal in my belly from watching Prince Bastian make that girl come with his lips on her neck has died down.

The man with the nose ring at the back of the auction hall, the sexy blonde guy in the corridor, and the prince with the intense gray eyes—they're all monsters. Nothing more. They'd happily suck these girls dry and spit them out, fuck with their heads until they can't give anymore, then kill them.

It's what they do.

It's what they *all* do.

Even the strongest tributes fall victim to the cycle. The girl with the hard gaze, who hasn't given her name and probably won't, got out twice and came back for a third go. She likes money, she says, but I know there's more to it than that.

She probably came once to get enough to get ahead, then was torn down again by the city. A city the vampires run, in every way that means anything. Her only chance to break the cycle is to get paid and get the fuck out of Maryland. She knows it too. I can see it all over her face. Something's keeping her here. Something's keeping us all here—mostly pretty lies and distractions.

Reality is brutal. But it's all that matters.

I only half-listen to the conversation swirling around me at the table. Winona is smoothing things over, explaining how even codependent women can pull strings or some shit. Jessica looks pissed. Good. That's better than giving up and rolling over for these creeps. Chelsea looks like she just realized how badly she's fucked herself by signing that goddamn contact, but she seems to be doing a good job of talking herself into being okay with it.

A few moments later, there's a stir by the door. Vampires and humans alike turn to look at the group of bare-chested men who have just been herded through the doorway by a trio of men about the same age and pallor as Anastasyia. The male tributes have all been oiled from the collar bone down. They look like a bunch of rotisserie chickens ready to be skewered. In a way, I guess they are.

They start moving toward a set of tables on the opposite side of the room. As they do, my heart jumps in my chest. There he is, the second one from the end.

Nathan.

CHAPTER SEVEN

OH GOD, he looks like shit.

My brother is so skinny. His eyes are sunken, haunted in rings of black and blue.

I'm not a big fan of guilt, though it seems to like following me around like a shadow I can never get rid of. I keep it at bay as much as possible. When people die on my watch, murdered by vamps before I can stop it, I pour out a drink for them and fuck or fight through the pain. I fuel myself with it, but I don't ever, *ever* let it take over.

Not until now.

Just looking at my older brother hurts my heart.

How did he fall so fucking far without me noticing? Dammit, that's not true. I *did* notice. I noticed, and I hoped he would pull himself out of it. I thought I'd done all I could, and that maybe my ever-present assistance was just keeping him dependent, keeping him from pulling himself up and sorting his shit out.

But maybe it wasn't that. Maybe I really just didn't want to help him anymore. If I wasn't already sitting, that thought would bring me to my knees, but I can't dismiss it just because it hurts. Helping him hurt too. But I should have taken that pain. I should have trusted in my own strength instead of betting the house on Nathan's ability to see the light from rock bottom.

I was wrong. I know that now, and dammit, if I could go back in time and do things differently, I would.

I would've *made* him move in with me. I would have worked harder, earned more, and moved us both out of this shithole of a city. Somewhere nice. Quiet. Someplace where he wouldn't have the chance to get into any of this shit.

That's what I should have done, and I swear if we ever get out of here, that's what I'm going to do.

I tear my gaze away from him and burn off the encroaching tears with sheer willpower. Nobody saw them, I don't think, and I can't afford to have an emotional reaction like that again. I can't let anybody know that I know him, or the vampires will get suspicious.

A sudden thought strikes me, sending chills through my heart.

Has anyone ever tried this before? Gone into the nest after one of their own? Are the vamps expecting me to do this? Do they know that their new male tribute is related to the one who keeps hunting them down?

No. Not possible. If they knew that, they'd know who I am, and they never would've let me inside these walls.

I slow my breathing, and once I'm sure I've got myself under control, I risk another glance at the male tributes. I was wrong before. They're not heading toward the empty tables that I assume are for them. Instead, they're being led toward the high table.

"Oh, wow. They're hot," Chelsea breathes.

Winona glances at her with something between disgust and disappointment. "Don't make eyes at the help, you idiot. They are nothing to you, you get me? You're after a vampire. With your"—she waves her fingers in a figure eight through the air—"physique, you might shoot for the lower end of the spectrum. Maybe a guard or the auctioneer. But never go after the male tributes. They're *human*. They aren't why you're here."

"Why do you care what she does?" Jessica asks with a frown. "Isn't it just less competition for you?"

Winona sniffs. "Slumming like that brings down everybody's market value, sweetheart. I refuse to have my reputation tarnished by association."

Chelsea blushes a bright, unhealthy red and looks down, muttering under her breath. I watch the tributes subtly, trying to keep my face half-hidden behind Jessica's head. I need to get a sense of how Nathan is doing, but I don't want him to see me yet.

Of course, as soon as I have that thought, I fucking jinx myself. Nathan's halfway up the platform steps when he glances around the room, and I can tell the exact moment when he spots me. His eyes go wide, and for a second, he looks like he's going to step out of line and run across the room toward me.

No. Don't move, I pray silently, my stomach knotting itself so tightly I'm sure I'll never be able to get food inside it again. *Stay. Shut up. Don't say a goddamn word, Nathan. If you value your life or mine, you'll keep your mouth shut.*

I turn away from him and giggle in Chelsea's direction, loud enough to carry but not so loud as to be unnatural. I don't know what the fuck she just said or if it was even remotely funny, but I don't care.

Read the signs, Nathan. For God's sake, play it cool.

"Nothing wrong with looking," I tell the still-blushing Chelsea. "Some of them are really cute."

My heart is thudding a million beats a minute as Anastasyia moves toward us, waving us out of our seats.

"Come, come," she says. "Smooth procession, come now. I thought Arthur would communicate beforehand to make this a nice coordinated effort, but I guess he's still upset that more female tributes were chosen in this round than male ones. I always tell him it's not up to me, so it's really not my fault, but he just will not let it go. Come on, shortest to tallest. We're behind, but don't look hurried. Decorum, decorum, smile girls!"

We all stand, and I get shuffled around, passed backward as the shorter girls jockey for position. Only Winona and the returning victim are behind me. We're led to the opposite end of the high table from the men, and the matron starts up the stairs just as the male tributes are settling into position before the prince.

Every one of the men is looking at the vampire court seated behind the table—every one except Nathan. He's looking right at me. I can feel his gaze burning into my face and I'm trying very, very hard not to look back at him.

We're lined up in front of the high table before I'm done wrestling myself under control. My heart is flip-flopping like a fish on the bottom of a boat as the shortest male and shortest female tributes stand next to each other, creating a clear view between Nathan and me. Anastasyia and the male tribute's—patron, I guess?—step forward as one.

"The new tributes, your highness," Anastasyia says, sinking into a deep curtsy. "And a wonderful batch they are too."

"Not nearly as wonderful as these new tributes." The man who I assume must be Arthur gestures to the men, bowing even more deeply. "Young and strong and impulsive, all of them."

Dammit, Nathan, stop staring at me. You're going to give us away.

The prince is looking at me. Not at the female tributes as a whole—no, his eyes are locked right on me. God fucking dammit. Bastian can probably hear my heart galloping like it's trying to bust out of my chest.

Nathan is still staring, and even as the weight of my brother's focus makes my skin itch, the prince narrows his eyes at me.

Shit.

He knows.

CHAPTER EIGHT

I EXPECT the prince to call me out, to drag me or Nathan or maybe both of us forward and make an example of us in front of everyone. But he doesn't. He stays silent, still looking at me intently, and for the first time, it occurs to me that maybe the vampire prince is staring at me for a different reason entirely. Maybe whatever has drawn his focus to me is a *good* thing—maybe it'll keep him from noticing the way Nathan is staring at me too.

Prince Bastian doesn't say a word as Anastasyia introduces us all, one by one. On the other side of the platform, Arthur is working his way through the male tributes, having them each say their names.

I grit my teeth as Nathan gives his real name. Did he learn nothing from me at all? Apparently not. At least he isn't staring anymore, but if he doesn't wipe that shocked look off his face, we're going to be caught anyway.

"And there you have it," Anastasyia says proudly as Arthur finishes. "All twenty of them."

The prince nods slowly, finally releasing me from his gaze to run his eyes over all of us. After a moment, he waves a hand, apparently dismissing us. Anastasyia bustles past me to the end of the line and leads us back to our table. The new male tributes are being led to the empty tables I expected them to go to earlier. The large dance floor is between us, but there's a direct line of sight from the male tables to our table.

Fantastic, more opportunities for Nathan to blow my cover.

"I don't think the prince liked us very much," Chelsea says glumly as we all find our seats again.

"Oh, don't worry about that," Anastasyia says briskly, smiling perfunctorily. "The prince has his moods, and not all of them are pleasant. If he disapproved of any of you, he would have had you taken away for—well, that doesn't matter. All that matters now is that you behave yourselves. The feast will begin in just a few minutes, so... well, just do as you're told, and everything will be fine. Now, I need to have a word with Arthur. That was a disastrous presentation."

She's off again a moment later, making a beeline toward the vampire man assigned to watch the new male tributes. I shoot a quick glance in Nathan's direction, glancing at him from beneath my eyelashes.

He looks stunned, staring at the table in front of him as if it might hold the answers to all of his many, many questions. I have to find a way to talk to him. He needs to know how to act and what to expect. He needs to know that his contract is over, null and void, the second I find a way out of this place, and he needs to be ready to run.

"Here you are, my pretties," a high, autumn-wind voice says. A vampire waitress pulls up to our table with a cartful of fruit. With super-human speed, she whips plates around the table, one to each of us. I poke at a grape suspiciously, and she laughs.

"Oh dear, do you really think we'd poison our own tributes? No, love, this is good, hearty food. A bit sweet—we do like our desserts too, you know. Eat up."

She disappears as quickly as she arrived, feeding the other female tributes before darting over to the male tributes' tables. It's hard to hear it all from this distance, but it sounds like she gives them a similar speech to the one she gave us, and Nathan turns a little green around the gills.

I can relate. Knowing that you're being fed only to be eaten is enough to kill your appetite forever.

Winona doesn't seem to have a problem with it. She's eating seductively, making eyes at some of the vampires—mostly the ones sitting nearest the high table—as she wraps her lips around her fingers to suck off the juice from the fruits.

I guess I have to admire the girl's ambition, but I can't say I understand it.

"Oh, these are the best berries I've ever had!" Chelsea's eyes light up, and she stuffs a berry in her mouth with no seductive artistry whatsoever. Winona spares a moment to wrinkle her nose in Chelsea's direction, then goes back to her hunt. Chelsea pays no attention to her. She's living in the moment, dissociating from the horrors around her in favor of relishing tidbits of misleading goodness. Like a sheep mowing the lawn on its way to the slaughter.

I'm torn between pity at her misfortune and fury at her stupidity. I stare at my fruit, wondering if it's the strain of the long as fuck day or some kind of spell that makes it look so appealing. And here I thought my appetite was dead. But there are predatory eyes watching me, watching all of us, checking the ingredients we fill our bodies with. I refuse to touch the plate.

In time, it's cleared away, replaced with a fragrant salad topped with some kind of fried meat and crumbles of fried and battered onions. My stomach growls audibly.

Fuck it. Maybe just a nibble. If I don't eat, it'll make me weak, and I'll regret it eventually.

But before I can reach my fork, a vampire sweeps silently up to the table. All the girls go still, as if collectively holding their breath.

"So nice to see you again, Elise," the man says in a voice like honeyed butter. "Come. I've missed your taste."

The girl who informed us all of the complexities of the vampire bond looks up blank-faced at the vampire, then allows him to take her hand and lead her from the table. She strolls casually beside him, her body betraying nothing of what's going on in her mind, and he takes her back to his table. The vampires sitting around it make welcoming noises to her, but she doesn't respond to any of them. She looks almost robotic, disinterested and detached. Worth emulating, perhaps.

My stomach curdles as the vampire laps at the pulse in her throat, then sinks his teeth into her. Her hard gaze softens a little, her hand reaching up to caress the back of his neck as he drinks from her. My skin prickles from nape to toes.

I expected her to remain stiff and disinterested throughout the feed, but she touches him like a lover.

Snatching up my fork, I turn away from the sight. I already got inexplicably turned on once tonight watching a vampire feed, and if it happens again, I think I might actually lose my fucking mind.

I'm still keeping half an eye on Nathan as I eat a few bites of the food in front of me. Nobody approaches him, though a lot of vampires—male and female alike—have taken other tributes from his table to drink from. He looks about as disinterested in his meal as I am. Or just as stubborn.

Actually, come to think of it, he hasn't been here that

long. It's entirely possible that he still has meth coursing through his veins, killing his appetite. Hell, the vampires might even be supplying it for him. I can't imagine they would want to deal with a tribute going through withdrawals.

But would they want to drink from him if he's still got drugs in his system? Maybe some would, but I bet there are purist vampires who like to "keep their temple clean" or whatever shit they say. So if he *is* still getting the remnants of it all out of his system, maybe that will keep him safe for a little while.

"We haven't met."

A voice at my right shoulder draws my attention, reminding me to focus on my own survival as much as Nathan's. I tense, fighting the instinct to tear the vampire to pieces, but when I glance at him, I realize he isn't talking to me. Chelsea looks up from her salad, her eyes wide and frightened.

"I'm Armand," the vampire says smoothly, reaching his hand out to her. "And you are?"

"Ch-Chelsea," she stutters, glancing at her half-finished salad with a look of regret.

He chuckles softly. "Don't worry, love. I'm not too proud to be seen sitting at the tribute table. Enjoy your meal—while I enjoy mine."

My eyes flare wide before I can stop them. *Oh God. He isn't going to—?*

Yes. Yes, he is. He sits in the empty chair beside her, leaning close and running his hands and tongue all over her neck. She's still holding her fork, but if he thinks she's actually going to be able to eat while he feeds on her, he's more batshit crazy or psychotic than most of these bloodsuckers. Or maybe he just doesn't care.

Ignoring her salad completely now, she stares at the ceiling, as if trying to escape to another place entirely in her mind. But when he finally leans in closer, setting his fangs into her neck as he bites her, she sucks in a breath and then moans.

I tell myself she's moaning in pain, but good fucking god, she sounds almost as aroused as the girl who came on Bastian's lap. This is her first time being bitten, and she looked nervous as hell a moment ago, but now her eyelids are fluttering, her jaw hanging open a little as her body undulates softly as if seeking something to rub against.

Forcing myself not to react to any of it, I sit stiffly, arms down at my sides, trying to look as bland and unappetizing as possible. It seems like it's working. The predator beside me doesn't even seem to be aware that I exist.

The courses keep coming, each more enticing than the last, but after a few bites of each, I lose my appetite—mainly because with every new course, another girl is pulled from the table. The music is light and festive, a celebration of death and dying, and with every passing moment the smell of blood and lust gets stronger. I get passed over again and again, but I still feel eyes on me.

Someone is watching me.

It's not Nathan anymore, thank fuck. His gaze is locked in curious horror on the slender female vampire straddling one of his table mates, her face buried deep in his neck.

But still, the agonizing, relentless pressure of someone's focus sits on my shoulders, making my skin prickle.

Reluctantly, I glance up at the high table. As soon as I do, all the food I ate turns to cement in my stomach.

Dammit. Of course the prince is still looking at me. He suspects something, I just know it.

But even as I lock eyes with Bastian, the prickling sensation on my skin doesn't go away. Someone else is looking at me, not just the prince. I turn my head the other way, peering past the pale but happy-looking Chelsea, and meet the gaze of the glowering bouncer punk I spotted at the auction.

I couldn't tell what color his eyes were in the darkness of the auction house, but beneath the glittering chandeliers, I can see that his irises are a deep, dark blue, almost black. His gaze burns like fire, and he doesn't look away when he sees me looking at him. His expression doesn't change at all, and I have no idea what he's thinking.

I wish I could read his mind, but I think I know what's on it.

Dinner à la *me*.

I tear my attention away from him, anxious to break the too-intense staring contest, but there's nothing to look at in this entire room but vampires doing their vampire thing and humans begging them to do it.

Pasting a listless look on my face, I scan the room, which turns out to be a big mistake when I catch sight of the gorgeous blond guy we ran into in the hallway. He's been watching me too, I think, but unlike the other two men, he grins when our eyes meet and starts walking over.

Fuck. Fucking fucking fuck.

So much for staying under the damn radar. I should've known I wouldn't be able to make it through an entire meal without getting fed on by someone, but I really don't know if I'm ready for this.

What'll it be, blondie? a panicked voice in my mind whispers. *Dark meat, or white?*

The joke falls flat even in my own head, because of course it does. Everything in me is screaming at me to find a stake and shove it through the nearest blackened heart. My pulse picks up as he comes closer.

"Hi," he says affably. "I'm Connor. We met in the hallway?"

"Right." I give him a tight smile. Why is he talking to me like I'm his equal? "Darcy."

He cocks his head to one side, his firelight eyes shining with enthusiasm. "Oh, like from *Pride and Prejudice*, right? Or, wait… wasn't that the guy's name? Not that that's a bad thing. I like guy names for girls."

I snort a laugh in spite of myself. He grins at me, clearly encouraged. Is he really trying to impress me right now? Must be a trendy vampire diet to hit on their food before taking a bite. Hell, maybe I'll try it myself one of these days and give my tuna sandwich some hilarious one-liners before I eat it.

"Hey, would you like to dance?" he asks suddenly, jerking me out of my spiraling thoughts.

I blink at him, then glance out at the dance floor. It's full of couples—*vampire* couples. All the tributes are busy snacking or being snacked on. Turning back to Connor, I raise an eyebrow at him.

"Is that even allowed? Us dancing together?"

His ears go a little pink as he follows my gaze out to the dance floor and around the room, then he shrugs. Those amber eyes of his darken ever so slightly as he shifts them back toward me. "It should be. It would be a crime not to ask a beautiful woman like you to dance. I've never been real good at crime."

Ugh, that was cute. Dammit all to hell.

Monsters shouldn't be allowed to be charming. They should be gross and scary and scaly, all teeth and bad breath, not baby-faced amateur comedians.

I should turn him down. Too much time with this one will have me questioning all of my concrete values. But vampires are competitive predators, and his attention has already lit me up like a beacon for those in search of an easy win. I can feel them circling me like wolves, waiting for their chance to strike.

Connor doesn't seem to be all that hungry. Not for blood, anyway. If anything, he seems almost... lonely.

Goddammit, Mikka, I said stop humanizing him!

I have to think of this in terms of tactical advantage and practical measures. A dance with this vampire will keep me out of reach of the others. Besides, I could use the distraction. My nerves are all the way on edge, raw with the urge to act and having no outlet to do so.

"Sure." I take a deep breath and then let it out, pushing my chair back to stand. "I'd love to dance."

CHAPTER NINE

There are way more eyes on me now as Connor leads me to the dance floor. Some curious, some pissed off, some —like the prince's—completely unreadable. I really wish Bastian would find something else to look at, he's creeping me out. Either eat me or don't, but quit salivating from afar. It's creepy as fuck.

Same goes for the stone-faced bouncer guy. I think he's still watching me too, but I don't glance his way to get confirmation. Honestly, I'd rather not know. I'd rather not think about it at the moment.

A waltz begins just as Connor and I reach the edge of the dance floor. Graceful couples sweep by us in perfect synchronicity, not even deigning to grace us with a glance. I'm pretty sure Connor is going to get in trouble for this later. I can't imagine what possessed him to ask me in the first place—but, shit, why do I care? It doesn't matter to me if they tear him limb from limb. One less vampire in Baltimore is always a good thing.

"Oh, I should have warned you," he says with a crooked little smile, looking at me out of the corners of his eyes. "I can't really dance—not the waltz, anyway. I can do a mean running man, though! A little boogey, maybe. Anything you'd see at a forty-year-old dad's barbecue, basically."

"I'm sure that'll go over well out here," I reply, letting a little gentle sarcasm creep into my voice as I watch the deadly beauties before us move in perfect time.

He chuckles and leads me out onto the floor, then slides his left hand awkwardly around my waist and grabs my hand with his right. I shake my head at him, a small gesture meant only for his eyes.

"Other way around," I whisper.

"Ah, fuck."

He grimaces and switches hands, then stares at the feet of the couples around us as he starts manhandling me back and forth across the dance floor. He stumbles on my foot and turns his breathtaking eyes back to me.

"Shit. I'm so, so sorry. I suck at this. I shouldn't have asked you to dance. I'm still getting used to all the vampire court customs. There are so many of them! I mean, they're more than happy to teach me, but there's so much to learn, and vampires don't really have a sense of urgency, you know. Side effect of being immortal, I guess."

My brows furrow as I listen to him, and I can feel myself staring, but I can't make myself stop.

What is it with this guy?

He looks so out of place here. He doesn't even *talk* like a vampire. It doesn't make any sense, but it's none of my business. If I start wondering about vampire backstories, I'm going to make a mess of my entire mission, now and for the rest of my life. I can't afford to give a shit.

On the other hand, I've never seen a vampire like him before. If the nest has started a suburban outreach program or something, I should probably know about it. At least that's the excuse I'm making for what I'm about to do.

"How did you end up like this?" I ask him, cursing myself inwardly for my curiosity.

"Like a terrible dancer?" He chuckles as he steps on my toes again.

"No. A vampire. You're... unexpected."

He flashes me a grin, then gestures toward the high table with a look that borders on hero worship.

"Bastian," he tells me, then quickly amends, "I'm sorry, *Prince* Bastian. It's so weird to use titles and things like that, isn't it? I didn't even call my doctor 'doctor' when I was human, I called him Paul. Anyway, Bastian—*Prince* Bastian, dammit, I swear I'll get it right one of these days—he saved my life."

My heart sinks. I feel like I know where this is going. Connor got wrapped up in some kind of criminal activity, got pressured by a gang—probably one run by vampires—and made a deal with another vampire to get out of it. That's always how these things go.

"I was hit by a car," he says quietly, breaking me out of my thoughts.

I look up at him, startled. That wasn't what I was expecting at all.

"A... a car?"

He nods somberly. "Yup. Downtown Baltimore, one rainy night, I was walking home from work. You know how the sidewalk sort of just disappears sometimes? I wasn't paying attention, and I stepped off a little awkwardly. Would have gotten away with nothing worse than a twisted ankle if that car hadn't come flying around the corner. I didn't even see the headlights until it was right on top of me. Crushed my chest."

He shudders at the memory, and I rub his shoulder comfortingly for a second before I catch myself. This is exactly what I was afraid of. He's too damn *pure* to be a vampire, the confusing bastard. He sighs heavily and shoots me a grateful smile.

"It was a hit and run with no witnesses. Nobody to call an ambulance. And honestly, even if someone had called nine-one-one, I would've been long gone before the ambulance got there. I knew I was dying. I was drowning in my own blood, and my heart couldn't seem to find a rhythm. Kind of like my feet."

There's that self-deprecating grin again. How can he joke about this?

"After the initial burst of pain, I couldn't feel anything," he continues. "Couldn't hear anything. Darkness was creeping in around my vision. Just as the world shrank down to two little pinpoint dots, I tasted blood in my mouth. I thought it was mine, at first. But the more I tasted, the stronger I felt."

He twirls me around, out of sync with the rest of the dancers, but doesn't drop me or step on my toes. He beams, thrilled at his success. I smile at him encouragingly and tell myself it's just the part I'm playing. I have to be nice to him, because that's what blood tributes are supposed to do. They're here to serve the vampires.

"It was really freaking weird too." Connor shakes his head, his nose scrunching up a little. "You ever popped a rib out of place? I never had, not until then. Even then, it was less of a pop and more of a crush. But when the bones grew back—or came back together, I guess. Grew again? I don't know exactly how it works. Anyway, it hurt like hell but in a satisfying kind of way, like popping a joint into place."

I don't try to fight the shudder that creeps down my spine. It seems like an appropriate reaction for the role I'm supposed to be playing anyway. I have to imagine an average human would be a bit grossed out by his story, so there's no reason to hide that I am too.

He smiles at me apologetically. "Sorry. Not the nicest thing to imagine, right? I won't even mention the nastier stuff. Anyway, the point is, I drank a bunch of Bastian's blood and re-inflated like a cartoon character. I had to spit out a few teeth afterward, but somehow I wasn't missing any. See?"

He grins wide, proving to me that his mouth is, in fact, intact.

"I see."

He chuckles, and the sound washes over me like warm waves on a beach. "So obviously I can't just go home or back to work after that. Bastian took me to a little coffee house on the corner and explained everything to me. Since I worked outside in a nursery—and since the place I was living was full of windows and roommates—it was safer for me to come here and live in the palace."

"So... he kidnapped you?" I ask. It's not the most polite question, but I don't care. Honestly, I'm partially trying to goad him into telling me how he really feels about all this. He's too damn cheerful.

Connor's eyes widen, and he looks truly shocked. "What? No! Bastian would never do something like that. He gave me a choice, but let's be honest—I've never been good at lying or skulking around keeping secrets. I would have gotten myself killed, either by telling the wrong person about all this or by forgetting about the whole can't-go-out-in-sunlight problem and stepping outside for coffee or something. This is way better for me. Bastian really, truly saved my life."

I give him a skeptical look. "You really think you'd forget about the sun problem?"

He nods earnestly. "Oh, yeah. I've forgotten things you wouldn't believe. You know those nightmares people have about going to school without their pants on?"

I wince. Vampires I can deal with, but public humiliation nightmares are next-level torture. "Yup."

"I've done that."

My mouth falls open a little on a choked laugh. "Really?"

He grins, his eyes sparkling. "Yeah. Twice, unfortunately. Once in middle school, and once in high school. Hell, I almost did it again before heading to work one day a year ago, but my roommate caught me before I left the house. I don't know, it's like my brain is always a couple steps ahead and slightly to the left of my body. Living in this palace is the only reason I don't wander into traffic in the middle of the day."

Chewing my lip, I consider his words as we glide around the dance floor. We're still not exactly moving with the beat of the music, but we've found a sort of rhythm that seems to work for us.

I don't know whether to believe him or not. He seems

smart enough, and I've already seen his sense of humor—but I've also witnessed his sense of direction, so his assertion isn't entirely unbelievable.

"And... are you okay with it?" I ask slowly, looking up to study his face.

"Been this way my whole life." He shrugs, a *what are you gonna do* expression passing over his features.

I huff another laugh. "No, I mean, being immortal. Having your life saved just to be turned into a killer."

His eyes widen in surprise, and my shoulders tense. *Shit.* I got too comfortable talking to him and let my guard down more than I should've. That's not a thing a good tribute would say. I want to take the words back, but I can't. Backpedaling would probably just make it worse. I'll have to figure out a way to spin this.

"A killer?" He looks a bit baffled again, then nods in understanding. "Oh, because I'm a vampire. That's just a rumor, honestly. A stereotype, I guess you could say. Vampires don't have to be killers. I mean, why would tributes come here willingly if they thought they were going to die inside this palace?"

He's giving me a big, concerned, doe-eyed look, the way a mentally healthy friend looks at you when you're making suicide jokes.

"Well, because they're in awe of vampires, of course. Just like I've always been," I say, letting myself lean a little closer to him as I soften my voice. Good. That's more like it. Much more like a real blood tribute would sound.

We turn, and over Connor's shoulder, I catch sight of Nathan looking up sharply.

"We are pretty awesome."

Connor grins and spins me a little, distracting me momentarily. I smile tightly at him before turning my attention back to Nathan, worry rising up in my throat like bile. A female vampire is leaning over the back of his chair, stroking his chest.

Don't fucking do it, bitch.

But even as the thought forms in my head, she drops her mouth to his neck. His eyes widen and his face goes a cold, clammy gray.

Every muscle in my body stiffens. Every instinct, every fiber, is telling me to run over there and kill the bitch who's eating my brother. I have to calm down. I fucking *have* to. If I break them up, I'll be painting a fat red target on both of our backs.

Kill her, now, the hunter's voice in my head screams, undeterred by logic or caution. *Kill the monster*.

But nobody will buy the dutiful tribute act if I do, not for a second. They'll have me executed on the spot, and maybe Nathan too.

I stumble in Connor's embrace, barely paying attention to the dance anymore. I keep sneaking glances over toward the men's' table, and every time I do, the vampire bitch is still latched on to my brother's throat.

You've had enough, stop drinking. That's too fucking much, dammit!

But I have to allow it. I'm going to have to let these bloodsuckers do the same thing to me, after all. A short-term sacrifice for a long-term win, like getting injured in a fight but still taking the vampire's head off. It's the same thing.

Still, for all my rational self-talk, I can't force my body to relax. I'm not trained for relaxation, I'm trained to take out vampires. Giving them an inch feels like losing a mile.

"Hey," Connor says gently. I snap my attention back to him and see concern shining in his eyes. "Are you okay?"

I nod—I think I nod—but I can't bring myself to speak. When I glance back over at Nathan, the vampire woman is finally done feeding, but now there's blood dripping down his neck to his shoulder. She's letting him bleed, why is she just letting him bleed? The blood trail makes it halfway down his chest before she intercepts it. She slides over him like a snake, lapping up the blood as it runs, taking her sweet time cleaning up the mess before she closes the holes.

Jesus. She was showing off. Proving her fucking power over him.

Playing with her food.

Hot fury lashes down my spine. I realize a moment too

late that I'm squeezing Connor's hand really, really hard. He follows my gaze.

"Oh. Beatrice," he mutters with a grimace. "I guess she grew up in the era of old-timey vampire movies, you know, big productions, heavy shock factor, lots of blood and sex. It doesn't harm her tributes, but it sure does freak out the new ones."

He spins us around so that I'm not looking at Nathan anymore, and I get the weird sense that he's trying to protect me from something he can tell upsets me. I meet his eyes again, but the obvious concern in his expression doesn't help my tension at all.

It's like having a tiger groom you—you never know when he might stop licking and decide to take a little taste.

"You should lie down," the blond man says gently. Empathy shines from his eyes, which crinkle a little around the corners as he gives me a wry smile. "This is a lot to take in. Trust me, I remember. My first night here, I threw up. It was all just too weird. But I'm used to it now. You'll get there too, I promise. I'll help you. Come on, I'll take you back to your room—if you remember how to get there, 'cause I definitely don't."

I smile half-heartedly at his joke, then shake my head, glancing around at the feast that's still going on around us. "I don't think I'm allowed to leave. Am I?"

He drapes an arm over my shoulder and leads me off the dance floor. "Let me tell you a secret, Darcy. As long as you're with a vampire, you can go wherever he takes you. And I'm fixin' to take you to your room."

"Oh. Um, okay."

I shoot Nathan one last glance as Connor steers me toward the door. My brother doesn't look gray or clammy anymore, but he doesn't look healthy either. His eyes are too bright and his skin is all flushed, the way he gets when he's been popping prescription amphetamines. I have to wonder again if they've been feeding his addictions while he feeds theirs.

Leaving the noise and blood behind us as we step out into the corridor doesn't help my mood at all. I want to run back in there and start taking monsters apart. Sure, I don't have my blades, but there were forks and knives on the tables. Even if they're just butter knives, I could do plenty of damage considering the amount of raw fury coursing through my veins. I can't remember the last time I walked away from a fight, and I don't like how it feels. Like surrender and passivity, like I'm *becoming* the woman I'm only supposed to be pretending to be.

I hate it.

Even more than that, I hate that I'm finding some semblance of comfort in Connor's mindless chatter.

"Okay, so I think we turn right here. I turned left once and ended up in some kind of armory, but it was like this medieval armory?" He chuckles. "I guess some of the vampires here like to keep things from their earlier lives or something. It's weird, right? Immortality? And the way some people cling to the past, even if that past was hundreds of years ago. I mean, I'm pretty sure Bastian is older than dirt, but he doesn't look it, does he?"

"I guess he doesn't," I murmur absently. The hairs on the back of my neck are sticking up, but they've been at attention all damn day. What I need is a good, bloody battle followed by a whole lot of raucous sex, but that's exactly what I can't do. Trying to stop my mind from churning, I tune back in to Connor's stream of chatter.

"—and I know you guys have kitchens and things back here, but the main kitchen makes some killer dishes."

Poor choice of phrasing, I think, but I keep my mouth closed.

"Like, they make this little fruit tart thing? It's tiny, but it's got more flavors in it than anything I've ever tasted before. It's fucking *amazing*. I mean, I don't really need to eat food anymore—it kind of makes my stomach hurt for a while, honestly—but damn, some of the things they put together are totally worth the pain." He grins at me, and I smile back at him.

I'm only playing a part, even though the smile came spontaneously. That just means I'm getting better at my role, right?

Eventually, after a few wrong turns and retracing our footsteps a couple times, we find my door. I open it cautiously. I wasn't given a key, so I assume courtesy is the only thing keeping other people out, and I've never relied on other people's courtesy for anything. I'm definitely not going to count on *manners* keeping me safe in a den of vampires.

A quick glance is enough to assure me that the room is clear. It will take a closer inspection to assure me that no one's gone through it, but I can do that after Connor leaves.

"I hope you feel better soon," he tells me, sincerity shining from his big brown eyes.

"Thank you." Weirdly enough, I sort of mean it. I can't trust him, but he did get me out of that fucking great hall.

He squeezes my hand and grins. "It'll get easier. I promise. Goodnight, Darcy."

"Goodnight."

Damn his charming face. He turns and walks away, but shoots a parting glance over his shoulder. I stare after him, unable to look away. He ambles like a man, like a *human*, without the practiced grace or hunter's gait I'm used to seeing. If I saw him on the street, I wouldn't even think to follow him.

Once he disappears around a corner, I step all the way into my room and shut the door firmly, pressing my back to it.

Don't get confused, Mikka. He's a vampire. A monster like the rest of them. Don't lose sight of that.

The image of Nathan getting snacked on pops into my head, and I have to pin myself to the door to keep from opening it and racing through the halls to find Beatrice and lop off her fucking head.

Adrenaline courses through me, making my hands shake with unspent energy.

Dammit.

This is going to be so much harder than I thought.

CHAPTER TEN

I SPEND the next several hours carefully pulling my weapons out of my dress and hand-stitching the lining back together. I try to fix the wardrobe drawer to hide my things, but it isn't as easy as I thought it would be. After a few rather loud mishaps, I decide to hide the weapons in the hollow space beneath the drawer instead, though they're much more difficult to get to in a hurry.

Of course, the only reason I would need to get to them in a hurry is if someone identified me as an assassin, which they would only do if they found the weapons, so they're better off down there anyway. The painstaking labor helps to calm me and passes the time.

I honestly have no idea what time of day it is anymore. I'm sure it won't take me long to get used to a nocturnal lifestyle, and for my internal clock to swap night for day and day for night. I should probably be exhausted right now, but I'm too wired up to sleep yet. Besides, there's still something I need to do.

Eventually, I hear the other tributes come down the hall. I count the doors as they close, until I'm certain that everybody is in their places.

Waiting is a skill I've had to learn, and I've gotten okay at it, but it isn't something I like to do. I have to stop myself from pacing my room, because if someone outside suspects that someone in here isn't sleeping, they're going to be paying attention. Since I've got nothing left to do to occupy my hands, I lie down on the bed and mentally map out the palace instead. There are large gaps in my knowledge, of course, but between what I know of the exterior and what I've seen of the interior, I can make some educated guesses.

Once I've gone over every corridor I walked through in my mind's eye at least twice, I sit up on the bed, cocking my head as I listen.

The palace has been silent for an hour at least, probably longer. By my best guess, the sun has been up for a couple hours by now—not that anyone down here would be able to tell.

Time to move.

I slide off the bed, then kick off my shoes. I'm still wearing the ridiculous peek-a-boo lace dress, but at least I can move in it. That's all that matters, really.

My door doesn't make a sound as I open it, and I let out a shaky breath. I pad down the hall, eyes and ears open for any whisper of movement, and stop near the end, where it intersects another corridor. A guard decked out in his punk bondage regalia is pacing away from me. I wait, controlling my heart and my breath.

He turns right, heading down the intersecting hallway. I dart forward on bare feet and speed in the opposite direction, whipping around a corner—eyes first, of course, to make sure it's clear—then stop short. The palace lights have been dimmed, giving me lots of shadows to work with, but shadows alone don't matter too much. It's the contrast I need. Even vampire eyes need a second to adjust. I've gotten really good at using that to my advantage.

There aren't as many guards patrolling the corridors as I would have expected. The one I dodged in the female tribute wing seems to be the only one posted there. There are two by the main staircase that Connor had so much trouble finding, but they're both bored and chatting. It's a breeze to sneak around behind them and duck through the passage under the stairs. I consider a surprise attack but manage to talk myself out of it. Missing guards are sure to raise alarms, and I can't let that happen.

I'm not going to assume anything, but I suspect if there's only one vampire guarding the girls, it's likely that there's only one guarding the guys. Once I'm out of earshot of the stairs, the palace around me grows deathly quiet. I take a few turns that lead to places I definitely don't want to be and have to double-back, but eventually I come to an area which is a mirror image of the female tributes' quarters. There's a guard leaning against one wall, scrolling through his phone. It would look odd to me if I hadn't just spent so much time with the surprisingly contemporary Connor. The weirdest part is that he manages to get reception down here, honestly.

I wait, still and silent, in a dark alcove. Eventually the guard sighs, stretches, and mumbles something under his breath. I have no idea what the words are, but a second later, he turns and heads down the hallway. Maybe he's supposed to make the rounds every once in a while.

Good. Gives me the opening I need.

I creep down the hallway, as silent as a human can possibly be. Identical doors line each wall, and I realize that there's one obstacle I didn't consider before I got this far. How the hell am I supposed to know which door is Nathan's? I stop moving and press my body against one wall, listening as hard as I can. Nothing. I take a few steps down, then press against the other wall. Still nothing.

Working my way slowly down the hall, I keep my ears open for any sound, any hint that will help me find Nathan. I hear the sound of a man crying, and for a second, hope rises inside me. But the voice is too rough to belong to my brother. Behind another door, someone sounds like he's muttering in his sleep, and in another room, I'm pretty sure a guy is jacking off.

Then I pick up a vague noise coming from a room a little farther down. I creep toward it and listen at the door.

"Stupid, stupid, stupid," a voice mutters.

My heart leaps. *Nathan.*

I tap on the door lightly, in our special rhythm—the one our mom always used to use when she woke us up for school. There's a lot I've forgotten about her over the years, but I remember that, and I hope like hell that he does too.

His voice cuts off cold, and I hear light footsteps on the floor before his door flies open. Nathan reaches out and drags me inside, closing the door behind me and crushing me in a giant, bony hug.

I'm so goddamn pissed at him. So frustrated that he let himself get this far into the shit, furious at him for not reaching out to me before it was too late. But he's here, he's whole, and—at least for the moment—he's safe. So I hug him back with everything I have, holding on to him like his life and mine depend on it.

"Mikka," he whispers, pulling away to look at my face. His green eyes are clear, but the dark smudges beneath them worry me. "Mikka, why are you here? You shouldn't have come."

"Shut up." It comes out sounding gentle, which pisses me off. I'm supposed to be angry at him, but once again, I find myself playing mother to my older brother. I breathe a cleansing sigh, pushing every irrelevant emotion away. "Tell me what happened. Every last detail."

His hands drop to his sides, and he starts pacing. "I was an idiot," he says bluntly.

"Yeah, I kind of got that from the 'stupid, stupid, stupid.' Give me specifics."

He shoots me a crooked smile. "I've missed getting yelled at." When I roll my eyes, he grins and holds his hands up. "Okay, sorry. I chose to come here."

My mouth drops open. "You *what?*"

He shrugs in his rolling, irregular way. "I was in the hole with a dealer. I was supposed to run some product for him, but I was living—well, you know where I was living. Somebody ripped me off. Stole ten grand worth of blow. Dealer assumes I used it all myself or sold it and kept the money, gives me forty-eight hours to get him his cash."

I can feel a lecture building behind my tongue, but I save it. I can tell this story isn't anywhere near over yet. Nathan shoots me a tentative glance, probably trying to gauge how close I am to blowing my fucking lid, then barrels on.

"So I go see this guy I know and tell him my problem. He tells me he can't do ten, but he can do five, and he knows which horse is gonna win the next race. Swore up and down that it was a sure thing. I'm thinking cool, if it's a sure thing that means I can get the dude his money and still turn a profit, right?"

I really want to shake him right now. But I curl my hands into fists and nod instead. "Go on."

He grimaces nervously. "So I put the whole five thousand on this stupid horse. It loses. So now I'm fifteen grand in the hole, and I've got two really bad people pissed at me. Time's running out. I freak out right then and there, and some guy tells me to go see the guy who runs the track, says sometimes he'll let a desperate person do some job or other for him if they want to get their money back."

Dear god, this town is full of predators.

"Okay, how did that go?" *Like I don't already know.*

Nathan blows out a breath. "I talk to the guy. He seems reasonable. Tells me I'm not pretty enough to turn tricks for him, and he obviously can't trust me to move product, so there's just one last thing he can think of for me to do. He needs someone to carry a gun and flash it around a little bit to intimidate some guy he's dealing with down at the docks that night."

I barely swallow a groan. My brother won't even look at me now, and I don't fucking blame him.

"So I go," he says with a sigh. "And I carry the stupid thing like I'm supposed to, and I mean mug the guy he's dealing with, everything seems to be going just fine. I mean, I'm still looking at having to come up with five thousand dollars in eighteen hours, but that's better than ten, right?"

"Sure," I deadpan.

He clears his throat and gives me a shifty look. "So, um —the guy starts acting a little funny, trying to be all intimidating, and the track owner gives me the signal. So I rush the guy and point the gun in his face, shouting some shit I don't even remember. The guy—this fucking guy—he falls over. Gets scared, I guess, and just fucking falls over. He almost goes off the dock. The case he was carrying took a long trip off the pier."

"Oh, no." My head is starting to hurt, my pulse pounding in my temples like a drum. This would be almost funny if it wasn't so goddamn sad. "What was in it?"

Nathan shrugs miserably. "Whatever it was, it was apparently worth five hundred thousand dollars. Obviously the track dude pinned that on me. Let me tell you, going from ten to five hundred in three seconds will make you puke."

"You puked."

"All over the track dude's one-of-a-kind hand-made special-order Italian leather shoes," he admits.

"Goddammit, Nathan."

He nods, his lips pulling into a grimace, then brightens. "But it's okay! It's okay. Because I thought he was going to kill me right then and there, swear to god. But he decided to give me one last chance to redeem myself. He said he had an opportunity for me which would settle my debts with everybody, and would keep me out of trouble for years to come. He, um—sort of said it with malice, and I really thought I was going to be sold to some human traffickers or a cannibal or something. But it was just the vampires! Isn't that great?"

I stare at him until his face falls, watching the hopeful façade slowly melt away.

"I want you to think about that, Nathan," I say slowly. "Really, really think about that. You were afraid he would sell you to human traffickers or cannibals. And where did you end up?"

He slumps. "On the auction block."

"For what purpose?"

"To be drunk from. But they don't have to kill me to do it, so that's a plus, right?"

"Jesus Christ." I bury my face in my hands, smothering a groan.

"I'm sorry," my brother murmurs softly. "I really am, Mimi. But the way my life was going, I didn't see any other way out. I really didn't. Everything was going wrong for me, over and over and over again, and I kept dragging good people down with me. I couldn't keep doing that. I figure if I'm here, I can do the least amount of damage. It's like being in jail or rehab, but better because... well, I guess the food's better? Also, they'll give me bonus if I finish my contract."

"If?"

He shuffles around uneasily. "Well, I mean, it's a thirty-year contract, and I've put a lot of miles on this body. Plus, with all the blood-letting, I just don't know if..." He trails off, opening his hands helplessly. "That's why... Fuck, you really shouldn't have come here. I'm really fucking glad to see you, but this is something I have to do. It's the natural consequence of my actions. Isn't that what you used to tell me?"

I gape at him. "Yeah, when you were crying on the toilet because you were too high to take a shit for three weeks! This is a life sentence, Nathan. A. Life. Sentence. For what, losing some dirty money? None of those bastards even deserved to have that much cash. You losing it was *their* natural consequence. This? This is nothing more than manipulation. That whole story you just told me was like watching a rat follow a trail of peanut butter to a snap trap. You were set up."

He shakes his head. "No. I don't think so—"

"You don't? Then let me tell you something you don't know. The guy who owns the race track is a fucking vampire."

"I—" He breaks off, his jaw slowly falling open. "What?"

"Yup. I would bet—not you, obviously, you're never taking another bet again—but I would bet that the guy on the dock was a vampire too, and that there wasn't a goddamn thing in that case. Who did you get the loan from?"

Nathan scratched at the slight shadow of stubble on his face. "Skeezy Pete."

"Vampire. And the guy who wanted you to sell drugs for him?"

He swallows hard. "Dude named Steel-eye Sam."

I frown, thinking. "Okay, I don't know that one. But think about it, Nathan. You wouldn't have gone to Skeezy unless you were desperate. Skeezy's the one who sent you to the track. Someone at the track sent you upstairs. You were *funneled* here like a rat in a fucking maze. Can't you see that?"

My brother shakes his head, then drops it and shakes it some more. He sits down heavily on the bed and lets his arms dangle limply in front of him. I don't speak, just let him process everything.

After a few minutes, he straightens up and looks at me with a frightened sort of defiance.

"It doesn't matter if I was funneled or not," he says, like an idiot. "This was going to happen eventually. You know that. That's why you walked away from me when I wouldn't move in with you. So that you wouldn't get sucked down with me."

My heart feels like it cracks open in my chest, leaving the blood in my veins with nowhere to go. I don't know what hurts more—that he would even think that of me, or that on some level, maybe he's right.

I sit down on the bed next to him and bump my head gently against his. "I really thought you would pull yourself out of it if I gave you the chance."

"Come on, Mimi, you know me better than that. I'm not good at things the way you are. I fuck up everything I touch, no matter what I try. Even when I got sober, I still couldn't get my shit together. I'm—fucking hell, I'm tired of eating garbage. I'm tired of having to fight off rats when I'm trying to sleep. I'm tired of trusting people and getting screwed over."

He sighs, and it's such a *broken* sound that it makes tears burn the backs of my eyes.

"These people," he continues in a low voice. "These *vampires*. They aren't good people, but at least I know where I stand with them. I know exactly what I'm supposed to do because it's all there in black and white. They're giving me a home and a bed and good food, they're settling up my debts, they're taking care of me—and all I have to do for them is let them suck on my neck a little bit."

"Drink your blood," I correct him harshly.

"Whatever," he murmurs. "At least the holes don't stay." He touches his old track marks self-consciously.

Something twists in my stomach, and I straighten up suddenly and smack him across the back of his head. I swear I mean to do it lightly, but all the frustration I've been channeling all night makes it harder to pull my hit.

"Ow!" He jerks, reaching back to rub at his dark hair.

"I'm not going to let you sit here and martyr yourself," I say, holding his gaze as I lean toward him. "You're wrong when you say I shouldn't have come here. I'm not gonna abandon you. I'm going to get us both out of here."

"Mimi—"

"Don't." I hold up a hand to stop him. "You aren't thinking clearly, but I am. I'm under a contract with the vamps just like you are now, but that doesn't mean I'm going to stop fighting. They don't get to rig the game and win every time. *We* get to win this time. All we have to do is get out of here, and I can take you far away from here. Someplace they'll never find us. How about Canada? Or, I don't know, Portugal?"

He doesn't look excited. "It's not a good idea to go up against these guys," he insists. "They're really powerful."

"So am I," I growl. "Listen to me, Nathan. You just keep your head down. Don't draw any attention to yourself, don't go flirting with anybody, just keep to yourself. Be a statue. No making friends, no falling in love with vampires. Also, and I cannot stress this enough—do not talk to me in public. Don't even look at me if you can help it. You and I do not know each other, got it? Don't let anybody know that you know me, or that we're related."

He hesitates. My heart sinks as I watch the expression on his face crumple a little. "Fuck. You didn't tell someone already, did you?"

"No," he says quickly. "But I think that prince dude noticed me noticing you."

"He did. I looked at you too, and I know I shouldn't

have. But if we course-correct from here on out and are never seen talking or fraternizing with each other, he'll forget all about it. At most, he's probably worried that we're dating or something. They say that pregnant tributes are a pain in the ass to deal with."

Nathan makes a face. "Gross."

"Right?" My lips curl in a grimace. "But it's better to let him believe that you're a scorned lover than an idiot brother."

He narrows his eyes at me, then laughs, his tired eyes warming. "I really did miss you, you know."

"Yeah, yeah," I mutter, shoving at his shoulder affectionately. "I missed you too. Idiot."

He hugs me again, and I let myself cling to him for a few long seconds. He *is* an idiot. And a fuckup. But he's my brother, and I meant it when I said he doesn't deserve this. There's a lot of shit I've done wrong when it comes to Nathan, but I'm going to fix it all. Somehow.

After we break apart, I turn away quickly so he won't see the tears glistening in my eyes. He's enough of a mess already. I don't need him worrying about my emotional state and getting himself even more stressed out than he is.

I head over to the door and press my ear against it, listening intently, but I can't pick up any sounds in the hall.

Nathan shoves me aside gently and opens the door, sticks his head out in the hallway, and looks both ways. He mouths "clear" at me and gets out of the way so I can do my own check. He's right, it is clear. I don't look back to see if he's doing the I-told-you-so face. I already know he is.

I'm on high alert as I pad silently down the corridor back toward the female tributes' wing. As I creep past the closed doors, I realize that although Nathan and I were being quiet, we should've kept our voices even lower. I can hear the guy in the last room snoring, and I don't even have vampire-sharp hearing. Hopefully the guard didn't pass by on his rounds. But if he did and heard a woman's voice, I'm pretty sure he would've busted into the room.

That thought eases the knot of worry in my chest. I'm being careful, and the vampire guards definitely don't seem to be all that on-edge or alert. Probably because they know how tightly the whole palace is locked down.

Just as I turn down a hallway, leaving the men's wing behind, the hair at the back of my neck prickles.

I freeze, sensing something.

But before I have a second to figure out what it is or even to react at all, strong arms grab my shoulders.

CHAPTER ELEVEN

Yanked off-course and pinned against a wall, my first instinct is to smash my head into the face of whoever's holding me.

I barely restrain myself. All of my nerves are on fire, my muscles twisting with conflicting instincts, until I smell it. The coppery tang of blood, and something sweet and rich, like mulled wine.

Vampire.

My hunter's focus rises above everything else, allowing me to calm my heart and my breath as I zero in on my prey. *Prey* that just happens to have me pinned up against a wall, but I've been in worse spots and still won the fight in the end.

I lift my head to meet my captor's gaze and find myself staring at my own reflection in a pair of pale gray eyes. The same pale gray eyes that were watching me all freaking night.

Prince Bastian.

Fuck.

He's got me pinned in with his body. He isn't hurting me, but he's damn sure not letting me get away. He pulls back and cocks his head, looking at me curiously. Hell, I'd be looking at me sideways too. I can't remember the last time a vampire got the drop on me like this.

But this one is silent as the grave. I didn't hear him coming, didn't *sense* him coming. It's like he materialized out of thin fucking air.

"Your heartbeat was faster in the great hall, when your safety was guaranteed," he murmurs, his thick brows pulling together a little as he studies me. "Why aren't you more frightened now?"

Fuck. I don't know how to answer that. At least, not without explaining that I'm a vampire hunter in my other life and have trained my body to stay calm during a fight. *Think, bitch, think.*

"I—I was just so awed and overwhelmed before, with all the luxury and power and—" I'm not making any sense. That's fine, I'm supposed to be a senseless groupie, right? "And, um, all the vampires."

Bastian cocks an eyebrow and twists his mouth. "Awed and overwhelmed. Of course."

Yeah, he's not buying this for a second. He glances down the hallway, back the way I came from, then turns that icy stare back at me. "So awed and overwhelmed you had to take to the hallways, alone and unescorted, in the dead of night. What were you doing, tribute?"

He doesn't say it like a slur, but it sure feels like one. Maybe I'm projecting, but I don't care. Fuck this asshole.

"I was trying to find a bathroom." I know it's the wrong thing to say as soon as it's out of my mouth. He must be aware that Anastasyia shows all of the tributes where their bathrooms are right away.

He actually laughs. It's a surprisingly human sound, but that doesn't make it any less creepy. He cuts his laugh off short, giving me a flat glare. "Do you prefer urinals, then, or just the men who use them?"

Crap on a fucking popsicle stick. Okay, so he knows where I was. Play dumb. I cock my head to one side, then think better of it as his eyes flash quickly to the exposed flesh at my throat.

I straighten my head again, clenching my jaw. "What do you mean?"

He chuckles, and the sound pours over me like rolling thunder.

"I see everything, you know," he murmurs. "I watched as you fucked the male tributes with your eyes. You couldn't stop staring." He leans close to me, his breath brushing against my earlobe as he speaks in a low voice. "If that's the kind of satisfaction you're looking for, my bed is always open to you."

My stomach dips and sways sideways, as if I'm on the deck of a ship in the middle of a storm.

"I wouldn't be caught dead in your coffin," I hiss out through my teeth, the words slipping out before I can stop them.

My heart thumps hard, and I bite my tongue. I know I've made a mistake. *Again.* I've always had grit, determination, and anger on my side, but I'm never been the best at disguising my feelings, and it's been biting me in the ass all night. It's only a matter of time before it gets me killed. Any willing blood tribute would be thrilled to have the prince himself make them an offer like that, and I just threw it back in his face.

Bastian draws back a little, but not enough to let me go. "You surprise me, tribute."

"Stop calling me that. Please."

Both eyebrows go up now, and he coughs out a surprised laugh. "I wondered why no one drank from you at the celebration. I'm beginning to understand it now. Have you not experienced that yet, my feral little—well, what would you have me call you?"

Mikka. Fuck. No. "D-Darcy."

"Darcy, then. Have you never experienced a vampire's kiss?"

My heart, the fucking traitor, speeds up. The prince grins, sensing it, and moves in closer.

"Ah, I see," he murmurs, his breath caressing my neck like a physical touch. "Then you really don't know."

He's testing me. I'm sure of it. And if I fail this test, I doubt he'll even bother calling the guards in to deal with me. He'll probably kill me himself, right here in this dark hallway.

I tell myself to relax, but my body isn't listening. It's going to happen, the one thing I've been dodging for most of my life, and there isn't a damn thing I can do about it. My fingers curl against the wall behind me, my nails digging into the smooth stone to keep them from flying into his face. Every muscle is tense, waiting for that brutal moment.

Bastian leans closer to me, his large body and dominating presence overwhelming me. He seems to take up more space than his physical body could possibly encompass, like there's an aura around him that pulses in the air, affecting all the atoms between us.

His fangs trace along my jugular, cold and hard and sharp, but they don't penetrate my skin. Goosebumps rise up all over me, from my head to my toes, as my skin itself tries to defend against the attack—but still, he doesn't bite down.

Tongue and teeth tease my tender flesh as his body presses close against me. His teeth scrape over my neck, sending a shiver of anticipation down my spine.

I don't want it. I don't want this.

But I have to keep *telling* myself I don't want it, because his tongue and teeth and proximity are doing strange things to my body. My head feels too heavy, and it rolls away from him, lengthening my neck for his mouth. Shivers of dread change ever so subtly, morphing into something else entirely. That arousal I felt in the ballroom flares up again deep in my belly, making my clit throb as my neck warms under his attention.

He nips my ear, then trails his tongue back down to my shoulder, nipping me there too. His sharp teeth press against my skin hard enough for me to feel them, but they never penetrate it.

Dammit, get it over with! I scream at him inside my head. I can't take the fucking anticipation.

But that isn't what this feeling is, not really. It's... it's *want*. He's putting me under a spell with his touch, that's what this is. That has to be it. Because right now, for the first time in my life, I want him to bite me. I want him to taste me, want his fangs inside me.

Then the teasing stops abruptly.

My neck is still whole. There are no puncture wounds, not even closed ones. He never once bit down.

I open my eyes to find the prince stepping away from me, his expression unreadable. The long line of his nose and vicious cut of his cheekbones make him look like a statue of an angry deity. Even in the dimly lit hallway, his eyes are clearly visible, and I could almost swear I see lightning crackling in the storm gray of his irises. He fixes me with a hard look, any emotion he might be feeling hidden behind the stoic mask of his features.

"Get back to your room, Darcy."

And just like that, he turns and walks away.

I have to press my back against the wall to stay upright. Adrenaline and something else I can't quite name race through me, making me tremble and shake.

I know I'm lucky. I know he could've just as easily killed me as talked to me. He could've ripped my throat out and left me to bleed out in the corridor, gasping and choking until my last breath.

But instead, he did... nothing.

Why didn't he bite me?

CHAPTER TWELVE

A timid knock at my door wakes me after not nearly enough sleep. I throw on some clothes, if you can call them that, and answer it as fast as I can, not wanting to be caught half-dressed by Anastasyia or some other vampire.

But it's not the matron of our ward. It's Jessica, and she looks like hell.

"Hey." She gives me a wan, hopeful smile. "Um, sorry if you were still asleep, but we're all going to breakfast, and I was hoping you'd come too?"

She seems more resigned to all of this than she did yesterday, but somehow less sure of herself. I give her as reassuring a smile as I can manage.

"Sure," I tell her. "Just need a minute."

When I'm finished with enough morning functions to make me feel halfway human, I find her in the hallway with her back pressed against the wall and her arms tucked up to her chest, her fingers linked behind her head as if she's shielding her breasts and her neck. She straightens up when she sees me, though, and smiles.

"Winona said she'd save seats for us," she says. "She's really pleased about last night, I think. She's in a really good mood. Things must've gone well for her."

I have no response to that, so I don't try to come up with anything. Jessica and I walk to the dining hall in comfortable silence. I like that she doesn't feel the need to fill moments of quiet with pointless words.

Honestly, she seems like the kind of person I would have liked to be friends with on the outside. Not that I ever let anybody get that close—friends are nothing more than liabilities in my line of work—but if I allowed myself to have friends, she would make a good one.

The undead must be late risers. The great hall is mostly empty of vampires at this hour, but there are quite a few tributes already sitting at the tables when we enter. The whole vibe is much different than it was last night, the atmosphere more relaxed.

Most of my fellow newbies seem to have adjusted to the flipped schedule pretty easily—I guess it's not so hard to do when you never see the sun—and are already chattering on animatedly over their breakfasts. A cluster of giggles makes my head hurt. Of course it's coming from the table Jessica is leading me toward. I slide into my seat and the dark-haired girl sits down beside me. She seems to scoot her chair closer to mine as she moves it in toward the table, but maybe that's just in my head.

Does she think I can protect her somehow? Or is she especially scared of someone here? What's going on with her?

"You're just in time." Another one of the tributes whose name I'm pretty sure is Gretchen grins at us. Then she leans forward, keeping her voice low. "We were just rating some of the vampires, picking the ones we're most interested in. Status is easy, because it's already built in to the system. I mean, obviously Bastian is the top dog around here, but anybody at the high table would be a good match. So now we're moving on to pure looks. Who do you think is the best looking of the bunch?"

"Connor," Chelsea murmurs dreamily, then licks yogurt off her spoon. "He's so cute and so fit, and he's got that whole funny guy thing going on."

"Nah. He's too much of a pretty boy for my tastes," Elise puts in, surprising me. I didn't think she'd have an opinion about any of this, or *admit* to one anyway. She points with her spoon across the hall. "Rome."

I follow where she's pointing, and my heart leaps up into my throat. The broad-shouldered punk bouncer looking vamp is standing against the wall, sweeping a brutal glare across everyone in attendance for breakfast this "morning."

"Oh, he *is* a hottie." Winona purses her lips, glancing

around the table with a smug look. "But I heard he was in trouble with the Elders. You know, the vampire court that sits up at the high table with the prince."

Gretchen nods. "Yup. Just got back from banishment. Supposedly his punishment is over, but you know how it goes. Ex-cons always gonna be ex-cons to some people."

"What did he do to the Elders?" Another girl—Demi, I think—asks.

Gretchen shrugs, stealing another glance at Rome. "Who knows? Nobody'll talk about it, at least not to tributes. All I know is, the Elders still hold a grudge against him, and he's always got that scowl on his face—unless he's feeding." She waggles her eyebrows smugly.

Demi gasps. "Oh my god, did he feed on you last night?" she asks in a whisper.

Gretchen grins. "A lady never kisses and tells." She waits a beat, just long enough for Demi's face to fall in disappointment, then adds, "But I'm not a lady. Hell yeah, he fed on me. It was hot as hell too. God, I *love* the way he does it. Trust me, girls, you'll find your favorites."

Jessica is pushing her food around her plate, not eating any of it. That worries me, but the direction this conversation is going worries me more.

"Sure, he's good looking enough," Winona says dismissively. "But honestly, the bad boy type never gets anywhere in life. Neither do goody-two-shoes like Connor.

He's sweet and all, but the other vampires will walk all over him for all eternity. Now, Bastian—"

"We know, we know, he has all the power," Chelsea says, rolling her eyes.

Winona purses her lips. "What I was going to say is that if you're looking for the hottest man in the room whose attractiveness isn't dampened by a personality handicap, Bastian wins, hands down."

"Guess that depends on what you mean by a personality handicap," a girl I haven't met yet says. "I think refusing to bond is a pretty big handicap. Why fantasize about someone you can never have?"

"That's your problem, Ji-yoo," Winona shoots back. "You see 'impossible' as a fact. I, however, see it as a challenge. You can bet your ass that when the bonding ceremony rolls around, I'll be the one lying across Bastian's lap. You'll be lucky if a vampire *busboy* chooses to bond with you."

Ji-yoo pretends to cuss her out in Korean. I've picked up just enough of the language to recognize a grocery list when I hear it, and I hide my grin behind my hand. Winona obviously doesn't have a clue what Ji-yoo is saying, and she flushes bright red, her eyes flashing murderously. I'm waiting for her to launch herself across the table at the dark-haired woman—and honestly, I kind of want to see Ji-yoo take her—but she just sniffs instead.

"You could at least *pretend* to have some manners," she

says. "Unless you really want to lower your standards that much."

Ji-yoo rolls her eyes. I shoot an amused glance at Jessica, but she's still shoving things around on her plate. I don't think she even heard the exchange.

"So, Winona, who fed on you?" Elise asks with a wicked grin. She doesn't talk a lot, but this girl's got an edge to her. I like it. She's just my kind of bitch.

"Oh." Winona shrugs, turning her nose up. "Nobody important. But the important ones will come."

"Guess so. You can't go anywhere but up." Elise smirks.

Winona's red face darkens a few extra shades and she busies herself with her food instead of responding.

Gretchen glances at Ji-yoo. "How 'bout you?"

Ji-yoo grins, tossing her sleek black hair over her shoulder. "Connor and Bastian."

"Ooh, a twofer," Demi says excitedly. "I got Frederick and Gabriel, which wasn't too bad."

"Gabriel's a sweetheart." Gretchen smiles almost fondly, making my stomach turn a little.

"I can't remember any of their names," Chelsea says, her voice a bit too bright. There's a strain in it, but she's trying to hid it. "But they all gave me desserts after."

"All?" Winona asks sharply. "How many?"

"Um... four? No, five. I was really dizzy by the end of

the night." She laughs quietly, looking down at the table. "But it was probably just all the sugar."

Sure it was. Keep telling yourself that, kid.

Jessica still hasn't said anything. She hasn't eaten anything either. I frown and touch her shoulder. She jumps hard enough for her knees to hit the table.

"Hey." I hold up my hands, alarmed. "Are you okay?"

She nods, but her hands are shaking. I drop my voice as the conversation continues around us, voices blending together. "Did someone feed from you last night?"

Jessica nods again, trembling harder. I narrow my eyes. She was plenty scared and freaked out the last time I saw her yesterday, but it wasn't like this. Now she looks... traumatized.

"Who?" I demand. "Who was it?"

She doesn't answer me, but her eyes slide sideways as a hulking shadow falls over our table. She turns even paler, her hands clenching into fists around the tablecloth. I look up to see a broad-shouldered man with bad posture and a shaved head glaring down over the table with unnaturally blue eyes. His features alone—high cheekbones, full lips, and regal nose—should make him attractive, but they sit wrong on his skull somehow.

"You," he says, pointing at me. "Come with me."

Jessica gives me a look I recognize from years of foster-shuffling, and my stomach clenches.

Pity.

Fuck. This must be the guy who bit her last night. As much as I didn't want to go with this asshole before, I really don't want to go now. I don't know her all that well, but Jessica strikes me as a reasonably strong person. She got over her tears and rallied last night, yet this vampires has rendered her shaky and speechless—and not in a good way.

But I don't really have a choice, do I?

The vampire's heavy brows lower over his glowering eyes when I hesitate, and I stand up quickly before he can lose his temper.

He doesn't waste a word on me, just grabs me by the elbow and hustles me through the room like he's got a train to catch. I drag my feet a little bit on purpose. I don't like being manhandled this way, and he hasn't earned anything even close to obedience from me. I can't openly disobey or fight him, but I don't have to just go along with him like a meek little doll.

He takes me to a little room down the corridor from the dining hall and tosses me inside carelessly, releasing my arm so fast I have to stumble to keep my feet under me.

"What, no introduction?" I ask dryly, even as my heart thumps heavily against my ribs.

Sass will definitely not help this situation, but I can't stop myself. I'm nervous and tense, and the way he's glowering at me isn't helping at all.

The vampire doesn't answer me. He pushes at the door, although it doesn't close all the way. Not that it matters. It's not like help would come if I screamed, not in this place. His shoulders round as he advances on me like the great hulking predator he is, light blue eyes flashing with hunger and malice.

The second he reaches me, he shoves my shoulders against the wall and pulls my head to the side hard enough to make my neck pop. I hiss out a breath, grimacing in pain.

He doesn't bother priming my skin. He doesn't even give me a warning.

He just bites, *hard*, approximately where my jugular is but just off-center enough that I can feel the hot blood pool under my skin. He sucks it out savagely, ripping it from me, and every cell in my body rebels at the intrusion. My breakfast lurches in my stomach, threatening to rise up my throat.

It burns like a strangling fire, and he's pressing so hard it feels like he's trying to break my neck with his mouth. I can't relax, not even a little bit. My shoulders twitch, my hips squirm, and my hands curl into claw-like fists, no matter how hard I try to stay still. I can't calm down, my heart is racing.

I've been hurt worse in the field. I can take this.

That's what I keep trying to tell myself, but it's not helping. This is different. It's not the heat of battle, and I'm not allowed to fight back.

He's ripping my life force away, stealing something

from me that I should never have to give up. I'm having trouble seeing as pain explodes like black stars in my vision, and my head is pounding in time with his vicious, thirsty mouth.

I can't fight it anymore, I can't keep my mouth shut—a cry escapes my lips, thin and hoarse. He doesn't care though. If anything, he just starts sucking at my neck harder, like he's determined to pull out every drop.

"James!" A deep, gruff voice cuts through the air, cracking like a whip. "Let her go."

CHAPTER THIRTEEN

I ALMOST THROW up when James yanks his fangs from my neck. It hurts even worse than when he bit down.

His mouth is smeared with blood, staining his lips bright red. It's dripping off his teeth and chin like he's some kind of fucking animal. And it's still pouring out of me. He never closed the holes.

He turns toward the door, and I follow his gaze to find the owner of the voice. A ripple of shock washes through me when I see Rome standing in the doorway. His broad-shouldered frame seems to take up nearly the entire thing, and his blue-black eyes are focused on James. I swallow hard and immediately regret it as the pressure pushes blood out of me faster.

"What the fuck do you want?" James growls. "Can't you see I'm feeding?"

"Is that what you call what you're doing?" Rome shoots back, his voice hard.

"I don't have to listen to you." James practically spits the words out, spattering flecks of blood everywhere as he talks. "It's not like anyone around here respects you anymore anyway."

Rome steps forward, radiating intimidation. *Real* intimidation, not the hulking mess this animal was posing with.

"I would be shocked if anyone respects you either," he growls. "You look like a pig at a fucking trough when you feed. It's disgusting."

The animal standing in front of me flushes, curling his lip at Rome. As much as he claims not to care what the other vampire thinks, the insult obviously got under his skin. My heart flutters weakly as alarm bells go off inside my mind. James obviously has issues controlling his temper, and there are two possible hotheaded responses to Rome's words—one of which would end with my head flying across the room. I'm too scared to feel properly relieved when he chooses the other option. He backs away from me and gestures at the mess on my neck, giving a mocking little flourish of his hand.

"You wanna show me how it's done, big guy? Be my fucking guest."

James crosses his arms defiantly and cocks his bloody chin up at Rome, his ice-blue eyes glinting with petty fury.

I'm dizzy and sick, but I meet Rome's eyes as his gaze flicks to me, determined not to show more fear than I already have. I can see the heat and hunger in his dark eyes, but there's something else too. I can't quite believe that it's... *concern*. I'm going to chalk that illusion up to wishful thinking.

He doesn't move for a long moment, and I can't decide whether I hope he'll accept James's challenge or not. On the one hand, the idea of another vampire feeding on me right now, drinking from the shredded holes in my neck, makes me feel like I might vomit. On the other hand, if he says "fuck it" and leaves, I'll be alone with James again.

And I'm not sure I could survive that at this point, even if I fight back.

When Rome nods slowly, my heart lurches. He walks over to me, and my knees shake so hard as he approaches that they threaten to come out from under me. I can't take this kind of pain again, not without a damn weapon in my hand. I expect him to go for my throat right away, the way Jack the fucking Ripper did, but he takes my chin in his hand instead and tilts my gaze up to meet his.

His irises are dark, so dark they're almost black—but from this close, I can see shades of blue and something like violet in them. India ink spilled on a kaleidoscope under a puddle of oil after a heavy rain.

Fuck, I'm losing it.

Keep your shit together, Mikka. It's not that much blood, dammit.

"What's your name?" he asks me softly.

"Darcy," I murmur. It's becoming like second nature now to give that answer. Shit, am I bonding with my spur of the moment stripper name? God forbid.

"My name is Rome. It's nice to meet you, Darcy. I won't hurt you."

Yeah, sure you won't.

Instead of saying that out loud, I let my gaze slip from his, down to where the floor meets the wall. It's a passive gesture, and it doesn't sit right with me. I hate this, all of it. It's fucking with me so much worse than I ever imagined it would. I haven't felt this helpless since I was a kid. Mostly because I've had knives in my hands ever since I knew how to use them, and I could always fight my way out of a tight spot.

Not this time. Maybe not ever again.

Keeping my chin tilted up, Rome drops his face to my neck. I suck in a short breath, bracing myself for more pain and that horrible wrenching feeling of having blood sucked from my body too fast.

But he still doesn't bite me.

Instead, he *licks* me.

He's licking my neck clean, I realize with a jolt. I feel like a wounded stray, and it takes everything in me not to whimper as I feel the wounds close under his magic touch.

I've seen vampires do this after biting before, but I've never experienced it and had no idea what it felt like. My skin tingles a little as whatever it is in vampire saliva that gives it healing properties goes to work. The sharp pain subsides, soothed away by the warm, sure strokes of his tongue.

After a while, he moves his mouth away, and his large, strong hands come to rest on my sore neck. He rubs it gently, working out the knots left there from James's rough handling, then gently tips my head the other way. The stretch feels amazing, and my eyelids droop a little.

Dropping his head once more, Rome breathes on my skin, tracing his tongue over my neck, pressing it against my pulse. His hands rest on my hips as he presses his lips against my throat, teasing me with his fangs, giving just a little pressure without penetrating. He works his lips and teeth and tongue up and down the line of my neck, from ear to shoulder and back again, until my skin is hot and my heart beats hard. The heat spreads as he finds a spot he likes and presses just a bit harder, sending warmth dripping down my neck, down my body, into my belly and between my legs.

I gasp when he finally penetrates my skin, but it's not from pain. The sensation isn't any more painful than a piercing or a tattoo—nothing like when James tore at me like a dog with a bone. There's a different feeling this time, more powerful than pain, more powerful than anything I can remember.

It's primal.

Intimate.

Heat swirls through me, and my head rolls back, giving Rome even more access. I groan as my pulse beats hard in my throat, the heavy throb echoing in my core.

Rome's hands are hot against me, pulling me closer. One presses into my back, holding me tight against him. His powerful thighs press against mine as he runs his other hand up my body, over my ribcage, brushing against my breast without actually caressing it. A little moan escapes me, and I realize with a shock that he's *hard*. The thickness of his cock pulses against my belly, and my body responds, an irresistible molten need swirling through the deepest parts of me.

My arms are around him, nails digging into his shoulders. I don't know when that happened, or when I started grinding against him, but I don't want to stop.

I don't ever want him to stop.

He's still drinking from me, and every soft pull on my throat might as well be his tongue on my clit or his cock inside me. My head starts to spin, and I tremble as I arch against him, seeking something that feels just out of reach.

No wonder they call orgasms "little death." He could kill me like this, and I'm not sure I'd even care.

But just as I've accepted a pleasurable death at Rome's mouth, he pulls away.

Licking me slowly and sensually, he closes the wounds

he's opened. His mouth lingers for a moment, breathing on the sensitive skin, then he kisses my neck tenderly and pulls away. The look on his face sends an aftershock through me—I've only ever seen him look hard and cold, coolly disinterested or pissed off. But none of those things describe the way he looks right now.

His expression is full of heat, full of passion. His eyes are even darker than before, his pupils dilating so much that they've squeezed his irises into tiny rings. He breathes a heavy sigh, and it catches in his throat.

My skin is flushed and hot. I'm staring at him, unblinking, unable to look away. I can't help it. I'm shocked and completely overwhelmed—I never imagined it could be like that.

I'm so turned on, so desperately close to coming. I'm afraid to take a step, afraid to even move, in case that little bit of friction sends me over the edge. I force my hands away from Rome's shoulders, because all I want to do is pull him close, grind on him some more, and let nature take its course from there.

"Are you all right?" he asks, his voice low and a little rough.

I nod dumbly, not trusting myself to make words right now. What could I possibly say besides *take me, I'm yours?*

Someone nearby scoffs, snapping the almost trance-like state I'm in. My body jerks slightly, the peak of arousal beginning to fade like waves drawing back on a beach as I glance over Rome's shoulder.

Oh, right, that fucking creep James. I forgot he was here.

"Very nice," he says sarcastically, his lips pulling back in a sneer. "But if we have to romance all our fucking blood bags, what's the point of even having them?"

Before Rome can answer, James slouches away, grumbling something about fast food and convenience stores.

I stop listening as soon as he passes through the doorway. I can barely hear a thing with my heart thundering in my ears, and I can't seem to find my equilibrium with Rome still gazing down at me.

I don't understand what just happened between us, but I know that on some level, it was much more dangerous than getting gnawed on by a vicious vamp.

CHAPTER FOURTEEN

As the buzz in my body slowly dies down, my rational brain switches frantically back on. I'm still turned on, terribly turned on, but at least I'm thinking semi-clearly again.

Rome wipes a few drops of blood off my shoulder, a few that he missed when cleaning up the other guy's mess, and frowns sternly at the stain on his thumb.

"Not all vampires are... civilized," he says, his mouth twisting in disgust. He turns those dark eyes back to mine, pinning me in place with the intensity of his gaze. "If any of them ever hurt you again, come tell me. I'll handle it."

I nod. I'm not planning on doing that at all, but I'll agree with him for now. He is, after all, the apex predator in the room. I really want to know what he did to get on everybody's bad side. How many brutal feedings did he have to interrupt to get himself banished from the palace?

How long was he gone before he was allowed to return, and who still holds a grudge?

These questions and more are pressing against my throat, but I swallow them. I can't afford to be curious about this man. I'm already in too deep, and this place is fucking with my emotions way more than I was prepared for. My feelings used to be my compass, but now they're spinning like a top, and I feel like I couldn't find north if my life depended on it.

Which it does, I remind myself firmly.

The only way to get out of this alive is to get out quickly. The longer I stay here, the worse all of this is going to get.

"Thank you," I say to Rome, shifting awkwardly. The fire inside me is down to its last embers now. If I can just get out of this room without touching him again, I should be able to put it out entirely. He nods his head to me in an almost gentlemanly sort of way and holds out an elbow.

"Let me take you back to the dining hall." Another look of irritation and anger darkens his features. "James never *has* let a tribute finish their meal."

I thank him again, wishing I had invested some of my education into learning how to make small talk. All I want to do is slip away from him, but I'm starting to understand the way things work around here. From the dining hall to the female tribute quarters, I'm free to move around. Anywhere else, I should have an escort.

So I let Rome take me back to the great hall. Once we're there, I wait until his back is turned to slip away. I don't really feel like going back to sit down with the other girls and facing a bombardment of questions. Given how unsettled my emotions are right now, I'm sure I'd end up saying something I couldn't take back. Knowing me, it would be something way out of the character I'm supposed to be playing, something snarky and harsh—an overcompensation for the conflict brewing inside me.

There's really only one way to handle this.

The vampire palace and everyone in it is throwing me off balance, fucking with me, *unraveling* me. And the only way to stop that is to get out.

I have to make headway on the next part of my rescue plan. I have to find a way out, and I have to do it now.

As I creep away from the dining hall, I see other tributes wandering around unattended. They all have the same glossed-over look on their faces, and it sends a shudder down my spine. Some of them grant me a dreamy smile as they pass, but their eyes don't quite focus when they look at me. It occurs to me that I've been doing this all wrong, trying to creep around when the vampires are sleeping—because when they're awake, they're busy feeding on tributes and apparently just dumping them wherever and letting them find their own way back.

Which is shitty of the vamps, but excellent for me. It gives me an easy way to blend in and not draw attention.

I try the look on as I gaze at my reflection in a small mirror hanging on a corridor wall. Vacant, unfocused eyes. Dreamy smile. Limp, listless arms. Loose legs. Looks like I just got fucked hard and put up wet.

Good.

A shiver runs through me as the memory of Rome's touch fills my senses, but I don't force it back like I usually would. That's the feeling, right there. That's the authenticity I need to get away with this.

I begin a spiral search pattern, looking for any weaknesses in the defenses. I've done plenty of recon on their lair from above ground, so I slowly start connecting what I've seen on the surface to what I'm now glimpsing below.

I finally figure out where all those smoke stacks on the surface are coming from—it's the vampires' various industries. Kitchens and smitheries and things I can't even guess at, nor do I want to. I wander into the kitchen at one point with that idiot smile plastered on my face and look up one of the pipes. It's at least forty feet tall, but only about fourteen inches across.

A tight fit, but not impossible. The problem is that down here, near the stoves and ovens, it's hot enough to make waves in the air around it—not to mention the crisscrossing metal grates every five feet or so. That's one hope dashed.

"Come on, girl. Out with you. You're not allowed in here."

The head cook chases me out of the kitchen with more patience than I would've expected, muttering about bubble-headed tributes, and I wander away.

Guards are posted at every intersection during the day, and they wander around their designated areas, always alert. Some of them snicker as I stumble by, giving each other looks I would expect to see on middle-school boys. Jesus. I guess being immortal means you never have to grow up.

Eventually, on one of my not-so-random wrong turns, I discover where the deliveries come in. It's a set of stairs a lot like the ones we came down when we were first brought into the palace, and at least half a dozen guards patrol the hallways around it. If I could ambush the guards, I might be able to use that as an escape route, but it'd be dicey.

That's about as far as I'm able to get before dinner. I don't even realize how much time has passed until Anastasyia finds me in the hallway and snags my elbow, pulling me after her. I quickly realize that she's rounding all of the tributes up like a mother hen, and I hurry through the corridors after her as she gathers the pack of girls.

Jessica slips up beside me, her hazel eyes wide as she nudges me with her elbow.

"Where were you?" she asks. "I thought that horrible James killed you."

I shudder. "No, he didn't . But not for lack of trying. Lack of skill, maybe."

She lets out a short, humorless laugh, but then her expression sobers. "He could bond with you, you know. Or me, or any of us. God, can you imagine being bound to him? All that brutality, all the time." She wraps her arms around herself and shudders. "And a magical element that makes you *want* it. Ugh."

"They aren't all like him," I tell her, trying to sound comforting. "Some of them are... nice."

She shoots me a suspicious look, looking equal parts shocked and horrified. "You sound like Winona."

"Ouch. Take it back," I say with a grin. "Before I start pointing out obvious shit like it's some scandalous discovery. If I start stealing that signature move from her, then you'll know I've *really* lost it."

Jessica grins as we both pick up our pace a little to keep from getting too far behind the pack. We walk in silence for a moment, then she shakes her head. "I'm really afraid of him."

"Well yeah, you should be." I squeeze her hand. "Just avoid him at all costs."

"How?"

I shrug. "Do it like Elise does, or hell, even Winona. She might be a bitch, but she's not a dumb bitch. Flirt with someone more powerful than—what's-his-name."

I know the fucker's name. There's no way I'll ever

forget it. But there's also no way I'll say it unless I absolutely have to.

Jessica snorts, looking a little less pallid and terrified than she did this morning. "So, basically everybody?"

"Exactly. The world is your oyster. Or... the underground is your brothel, or something. I don't know, I'm not good with analogies."

She chuckles softly, and the sound bursts a bubble of stress in my chest, sending relief coursing through me. I didn't know I was so worried about her until just now. Just another complication to add to my never-ending list of complications, dammit. But I don't really mind. With Winona playing mean girl and trying to push people around, and the rest of the girls mostly looking out for themselves, Jessica needs a friend in her corner—even if I am temporary.

Anastasyia leads us all back to the tribute wing and gives us twenty minutes to dress, reminding us to take advantage of the provided wardrobe and choose something beautiful.

I choose a gown that's gauzy and gossamer, with thin layers of lace in the skirt and a beaded bodice with a small strap that crosses over one shoulder. There's a split at my left leg that shows glimpses of my thighs and calves as the fabric billows lightly with every step. The entire thing is a very pale blue, so light that it's almost white. It's different than anything I've worn before, but I sort of like how it seems a bit incongruous with the rest of this place. I like not fitting in here.

Our matron is waiting for us when we step out of our rooms, and once the stragglers join our little group, she leads the way through the labyrinthine hallways back toward the great hall.

"Is this *another* celebration?" I ask as we step into the massive room. The band is onstage again, the dance floor polished to a blinding sheen, and there are fresh flowers everywhere. The high table is full of vampires—Elders and other important members of the court, presumably—and Bastian already has a girl in his lap.

"Oh, they get like this almost every night," Elise says, turning to look back at me. "They like to live like they're dying, because they never will."

That's what they think, I muse darkly.

One of these days, after I figure out how to get Nathan out of here, I'm going to use everything I've learned about them to wipe this whole place off the face of the earth.

I'm fairly certain at this point that our hosts aren't poisoning the food. That vampiress who served us last night was right; it wouldn't make sense to taint the herd before they're eaten. Besides, I'm starving. It's not from the walk around the palace—that wasn't nearly enough exercise to get me feeling this way. It's probably because I didn't eat much last night, and my breakfast was interrupted before I could finish.

That, and the fact that two vampires fed on me today.

I suppress a shudder at the thought of how much blood I've lost and take my seat. Unlike last night, I demolish every plate as fast as they can bring it to me, paying no attention to looking pretty while I do it. I can sit down and eat two large pizzas on my own after a tough hunt, so these fancy little dishes are nothing.

When I finally bother to glance up from my meal, I find Winona looking at me with thinly-veiled horror. I ignore her, but she gets more and more theatric about it until finally, exasperated, she bursts out with, "Oh my god. Do you need another fork?"

I pause with my mouth full, looking at her thoughtfully. "Sure. Give me yours, since you're not using it. What's the matter, didn't work up an appetite today?"

Her face flushes, and she falls silent, letting me go back to my food in peace. Jessica chuckles quietly, hiding a grin behind her hand. Gretchen is grinning too, but she's not bothering to hide it.

"Any of your royals take an interest in you yet, Winona?" she asks, still smirking.

Winona sniffs and turns up her nose. "I told you, it's only a matter of time. Patience is a virtue, you know."

I'm about to dig into my food again, second fork or no, when the hair on the back of my neck stands up.

There's a vampire approaching. I can feel him.

My spine stiffens as I glance around surreptitiously.

From the corner of my eye, I can see a huge, rough-looking vampire striding toward our table. His gaze is focused on me, and the expression on his broad face is hungry.

Fear washes through me as memories of this morning fill my head. He's coming to feed on me, I'm sure of it, just like James did this morning.

Okay, think, Mikka.

James could have killed me, but Rome stopped him. If I don't let this big guy take me out of the ballroom, Rome might intervene again. If I *do* let him take me out, maybe I could find a stray stake or something lying around. Fat chance.

Before I can talk myself into pulling a Buffy in the bathroom, someone else steps up to the table, blocking the big vampire from my sight. I glance up and allow myself a small, relieved smile as I take in Connor's familiar face. His blond hair is messier than usual, and his amber eyes gleam like warm honey in the light from the chandeliers.

"Might I have this dance, fair lady?" he asks in an over-the-top formal voice that almost sounds British, holding his hand out with a flourish.

"Why of course, good sir."

I grin at him, mimicking his voice. Pushing my almost-finished plate away, I lift my hand to his and let him twirl me out of my chair.

It wasn't hard to accept his offer. I tell myself that I simply prefer the devil I know—but deep down, I have to admit that I enjoy Connor's attention. I enjoy *Connor*. He makes me feel almost normal, and in a place like this, that's like finding water in the fucking desert.

Still, knowing that nothing and no one in this place is truly what they seem, I can't help but feel like his sweet face and gentle optimism have to be an illusion.

Like it's just a matter of time until the other shoe drops.

THE NEXT WEEK passes faster than I would like. I spend as much of every day as I can wandering the corridors of the palace, breaking up my recon with time spent in the great hall or the small lounge in the female tributes' wing with the other girls. I know I have to be seen doing other things to avoid drawing attention or suspicion as I search for a way out, but every minute that I'm not mapping out the palace feels like wasted time.

When we first arrived, Anastasyia said that the bonding ceremony was set to take place in a few weeks, so the clock is ticking. I have hope that neither Nathan nor I would be chosen by a vampire to become their blood-bonded human, but I don't like to rely on things like hope.

Which means I need to get us out of here before the ceremony happens.

I haven't found a way out yet, despite the hours I've

spent searching. It's starting to look like I'm going to have to fight or talk my way out of here—both foolish, neither likely to succeed. But there are still some parts of the palace I haven't seen yet, so maybe there's a route I haven't discovered yet. The sprawling palace bleeds into the old underground, and as such, it's filled with dead ends and random doorways that lead to nowhere.

Dinner every evening is a grand production, with dancing and music and a million courses. And every evening, Connor asks me to dance.

He's done the same thing each night since I first arrived, asking me to dance but never touching his fangs to me. I'm glad for the buffer between me and the other hungry vampires, who seem to be getting increasingly irritated that I'm never available. It's become a bit of a race to get to my table when dinner begins every night, but I pretend not to notice.

Tonight, Connor beats three vampires to my table to ask me to dance. I haven't even finished my salad yet, but I'm not about to argue. Still, my curiosity is getting the better of me.

I wait until he's twirled me to the far side of the dance floor, where the music from the band will hide my voice and I'll be too far away for anybody to read my lips.

"Why do you always ask me to dance?" I ask him once we're finally there.

He shrugs and gives me a lopsided grin. "Need the

practice. Wouldn't want to smash down some three-hundred-year-old woman's toes, right? Gotta practice with someone young and sturdy enough to take the abuse."

He winks at me, his eyes sparkling, but I level him with a skeptical look. I don't buy for a second that he's doing this just for the practice, and I let my disbelief etch itself all over my face.

Connor's grin fades, and he looks away, gazing out over the crowd of vampires milling around and between tribute tables. When he turns his face back to me, there's a somberness to his gaze I haven't seen in him before.

"It keeps you busy," he says quietly. "Keeps the others from feeding on you."

I fight against a frown. That doesn't make sense. He sounds almost protective, but that can't be right. All the vampires do the same thing, don't they?

They all feed on humans. It's part of the whole deal. Technically, any of them could feed on me anytime, and a few of them have if they manage to find me during the day, although I do my best to keep moving around and make myself scarce if there are any vamps around. Connor must feed on blood too, although I've never seen him drink from anyone during the feasts that take place nightly.

Is he possessive then, maybe? He wants to keep me for himself?

But that doesn't make sense either, since he's never so much as tried to kiss my neck.

"Why haven't *you* fed from me?" I ask abruptly. Too abruptly, I realize, as the tips of his ears turn pink.

He glances down at me without answering, his golden eyes warm. He looks almost shy. No, I decide as his eyelashes flutter against his cheeks for a moment—he *definitely* looks shy.

His gaze roves over my face for a moment, and then he pulls me a little closer, too close for a proper waltz.

"Would you like that?" he murmurs in my ear. "Do you want me to?"

My stomach flips. What the fuck? No, of course I don't.

But... yes.

Some part of me *does* want it. The part that the prince and Rome both tapped into somehow, the part of me that craves their touch like a suicidal cow being led to the slaughter. My breath is raspy, and I can feel Connor responding—half aroused, half timid, like he doesn't know if I'm turned on or afraid of him.

I'm not afraid of him, I know that much for sure. I also know that I'm supposed to be playing the role of an eager tribute, so my feelings don't really matter anyway.

Dragging in a breath, I bite my lip and nod. It's a mistake to meet his eyes as I do, because they darken with a blazing heat, and something in my body responds to it.

Changing course slightly, Connor dances me to the edge of the floor, then tucks my arm in his—a clumsy imitation of a classic gesture, but still kind of nice—and leads me through the crowd toward the large doors on one side of the room.

As we pass Nathan's table, I can't help stealing a quick peek at my brother. He's been much better about not looking at me or acknowledging me in public, and I do my best to ignore him too so that no one will realize we know each other, but I can't help worrying about him.

He's looking a bit better, the dark circles beneath his eyes fading a little, and I let out a relieved breath. Maybe the remnants of whatever drugs he was on are finally out of his system.

But even as I feel that weight lifting off my chest, I notice a female vampire crossing the room toward my brother with a ravenous, seductive look on her face. My stomach twists itself into knots all over again.

He may be clean, but he's still not safe.

CHAPTER FIFTEEN

We step out into the quiet corridor, and I do my best to shake off the parting image of the brunette bloodsucker making a beeline for Nathan.

Connor leads me a little way down the hall, looking as nervous and excited as a kid on prom night. Part of me wants to reassure him, which is stupid. What kind of vampire needs reassurance before he bites somebody?

Then again, what kind of vampire uses his food for dancing lessons? I might just have to accept that Connor isn't your average vamp.

I brace myself against the wall but smile at him.

Dammit all, I'm not his girlfriend, I'm his food.

But his breath catches in his throat as he licks his lips, and I can't look away from his gaze. His hands tremble slightly as he cups my face, turning my head aside to expose my throat. His breath is hot and fast on my skin.

Jesus, I feel like I'm deflowering a virgin. I never have known how to feel about that.

His lips linger lightly on my neck, right at my pulse. He kisses me softly and flicks his tongue against my skin—not like he's tasting it, but like he's feeling it. He's still so close to being human, it isn't fucking fair. It's too easy for me to pretend this is something it isn't.

My body is already buzzing with heat and adrenaline, but Connor hesitates, moving his mouth over me with agonizing slowness. I can't tell if he's teasing me or if he's working up his nerve. Either way, the waiting is beginning to fray my nerves.

I put my hands on his back, just over his hips, and press my body close to his. His breath deepens as he relaxes, and then I feel them—his sharp fangs scraping over my skin. Anticipation makes my stomach clench and my knees weak, and I grab him a little harder for support. His breath quickens again, but he's not hesitating anymore.

His teeth pierce my skin, more painful than Rome but far less so than James. He pauses after he's in and just... holds me. I allow myself to be comforted by his touch, his nearness, the barrier of him between me and the world—even though he's doing what the rest of the vampires would do if he gave them the chance.

It seems different, somehow, like getting bit by a friend. *Don't think like that, Mikka,* I remind myself angrily.

But before the thought can form into any kind of real

command, Connor starts drinking. Silvery pleasure runs through my veins, clouding my head and putting a heavy, warm weight low in my belly. He's gentle, holding me close, and doesn't let his hands drift too far. Still, I can feel what this is doing to him, and I have the urge to tease him with my hips, to grind against the hardness of his cock. What's wrong with me?

I restrain myself from moving too much, but I can't keep from enjoying it. There's some kind of magic that goes along with these voluntary feeds; something that makes them less horror and more foreplay. Arousal pulses deep inside me, and I forget about my own directive to keep still, allowing my fingers to drift into his hair.

Time passes at a slow, dreamy rate, and I can't tell how long it all lasts before he finally withdraws his teeth from my skin. After sliding out, he licks my wounds closed but doesn't pull away. Not much, anyway. He's still holding me close, his forehead almost touching mine and his eyes burning.

There's a bit of my blood on his lip. Without thinking, I run my thumb over it. He catches the tip of my thumb in his mouth, kisses it, and releases it back to me with a slow turn of his head. My clit throbs, my body practically straining toward his as he cages me in against the wall. I want him to do that again. I want him to do a hell of a lot more than that.

Before I can talk myself out of it, I tilt my head up even

more, closing the last small bit of space between us as I press my lips to his.

He responds instantly, holding me closer and kissing me back, his mouth hungry and warm. Every move is slow, deliberate, but I can feel the tension in him just below the surface.

He *wants* me, I realize, and not just for dinner.

When Connor finally breaks the kiss and pulls away, his eyes are bright. The fierce pull inside me that draws me to him against all my better instincts, reflects back at me from his gaze. He chuckles softly, his voice a little rough.

"I don't usually kiss someone after I feed from them, but... fuck, I really wanted to do that. I'm sure all the guys say this," he murmurs with a crooked half-smile as he raises my hand to his lips to kiss my knuckles. "But that's never happened before."

I open my mouth to say something—but what? My usual snappy comebacks to dudes who feed me lines in bars don't feel right, not with him standing there looking at me like I'm something precious.

When a few long seconds pass and I don't say anything, the tension between us begins to build again, as if fed by my silence. Connor's expression turns more serious and intense, and he starts to lean in again, moving in for another kiss as my heart thunders away inside me.

"May I cut in?"

The voice behind Connor is cool and smooth, deep

and precise. Even though I've only spoken to him once, I recognize who it is immediately.

Bastian.

Goose bumps prickle across my skin as my breath hitches. Connor's smile falls, and his shoulders tense as he draws back a little. He clearly wants to tell the prince to fuck off, but the "request" was more of a command, and we all know it. After a long pause, the blond man steps away from me but keeps his gaze fixed to mine.

"Are you okay?" he asks.

I get the distinct impression that if I say "no," he won't leave. He's asking if I'm okay with being alone with Bastian, and if I tell him I'm not... would he disobey a direct order from his prince?

I blink, stunned, but nod at him. I don't know how to feel about the protective look on Connor's face, and I'm not sure I want to start some shit between these two vampires. Normally, I'd love to watch two bloodsuckers fight it out, but it could only end badly in this case. It could risk blowing my cover, and more than that, I have a feeling Connor wouldn't last long in a fight against a vampire as powerful and experienced as Bastian.

The thought of watching this sweet, gentle man get his ass kicked makes my stomach twist unpleasantly, even if he is a vampire.

"Yeah. I'm okay," I manage to say. "Thanks."

Bastian waits for Connor's respectful—if terse—nod

before taking my arm. Connor hesitates again before reluctantly turning and heading back toward the great hall.

I assume we're going to follow him, heading back to the revelry and dining, but the prince sweeps me right past the big doors and on down the corridor. Memories of James's attack rush through me, bringing a sick wave of panic with them. I shut it down quickly, but not fast enough. Bastian cocks an eyebrow at me, then looks away, and I can tell he noticed the change in my demeanor. He doesn't comment on it, but I'm not sure that's better—because now I have no idea what he's thinking.

After guiding me through the corridors with a sure stride, he takes me to a door that I haven't explored yet. It matches every one of a dozen or more doors on this side of the hallway, and at first, I think it's just another little sitting room, like the one James dragged me into. But it opens into a narrow hall instead. From what I've mapped out in my head, I'd guess this hall cuts right through the heart of the palace.

Another narrow corridor cuts across this one, forming a cross. *Ha. How ironic*. On the far side of the intersection, there's an elevator, something I haven't seen anywhere else in the palace yet. There's a keypad in place of a call button, but it isn't made with steel buttons like some older keypads, which sucks. If it were, I might be able to guess the code based on the wear pattern. This one is a touchscreen, which I haven't learned any tricks for yet.

Bastian stands between me and the screen while he punches the code in. I can't see what he's pressing without making it obvious that I'm trying to, so I keep my peace, not wanting to draw suspicion. There will be other chances for me to try to glean the code. Or at least, there better be—because this elevator might be my best chance of getting out of here with Nathan.

A second later, the doors slide open without a sound, and he steps aside, gesturing for me to go in ahead of him. God, I wish he'd say something. I can't read his face or his body language. It's a lot harder to make my feet move when I don't know if I'm stepping into an ambush.

Apart from the metal doors, the elevator is glass. Not that it does me any good right now—there's nothing to see outside but the concrete shaft—but my heart leaps with excitement anyway. On the off chance that he's planning to take me above ground, it will show me where I am. And, possibly, a way to get out.

I try to appear perfectly innocent and only vaguely interested as the vampire prince follows me into the elevator and pushes a button. He grants me a small, tight smile, which is the most expressive I've seen his face be since he caught me wandering the halls on my first night here.

Shit. That's probably why he stole me away from Connor. He's probably taking me away to punish me for wandering around the other night.

I have to suppress a shudder at the thought. I don't know what vampire punishments look like, but I'm not in a hurry to find out.

My concerns take a back seat as we move higher and the concrete shaft gives way to city lights around us. We're in the sleek high-rise building that sits atop the vampires' lair, I realize, and the ambient light spills in through large windows.

Bastian glances at me, watching my expression as I take it all in. "We can't very well run our legitimate businesses from the underground," he tells me, his voice smooth as melted butter. "As much as the Elders would prefer it. We have too many of our own kind to take care of to allow ourselves to be surpassed by time and technology."

"So this building, it's—?"

"Our base of operations these days," he says. There's a touch of nostalgia around his eyes, or maybe I'm imagining it. "Perhaps not as dramatic as the palace below, but just as intimidating."

I frown. "Why would the Elders prefer to do business from the underground?"

He sighs. "Many of them are anchored in the past, I'm afraid. Immortality tends to affect different people differently. Some become obsessed with youth and novelty, desperate to feel as young as they look. Others..." He presses his lips together, his eyes going a little unfocused as if he's lost in some thought he isn't sharing. "I believe they are intimidated by progress, and so they fight to keep the world around them working as it did when they first felt power."

"Oh." I nod, not quite sure what to say.

A small smile pulls at his lips, making his face look a little less like it's been carved from stone. "They would prefer, I think, that I dispatch with dishonorable businessmen by beheadings in the throne room. Lawsuits strike them as being tedious and unreliable."

I fight the chuckle that almost bursts from my lips. The idea of Elon Musk or Bill Gates being called to task in a Victorian-era throne room is just too ridiculous. I mean, probably not Victorian, per se. Bastian can't possibly be *that* old.

When the elevator finally stops at the very top, we step out onto the roof and gaze down at the city below. The air is fresh up here, in a way that I've never tasted it. I inhale deeply through my nose, closing my eyes to revel in the crisp clean feel of it. Down below, a breath like that would have choked me.

I open my eyes to see Bastian watching me. His expression is stony and inscrutable again, but his storm cloud eyes are warm.

"That's why I come up here," he says softly. "I remember when I could walk the streets at night and taste the harbor in the air. Before exhaust fumes filled the world with poison."

Before exhaust fumes? I can't remember when cars replaced horses as the way to travel, but I know it wasn't yesterday. Curious, I narrow my eyes at him. I know I shouldn't ask, but what the hell. Worst he can do is kill me.

"How old are you?"

Bastian raises a brow, looking surprised, but not necessarily offended.

"Let's see," he murmurs, as though he has to calculate it. "As of this year—I am five hundred years old."

I blink, trying to wrap my head around that. "I never was much good at history in school," I tell him. "But I'm pretty sure that means you're older than the US."

He nods, sighs, and gestures at the city below. "Everything you see around us? I watched it grow. I was here when the underground was on the surface, or just beneath it. I watched this city rise, fall, and rise once more. It's falling again. I'm sure you see that."

Awed as I am in the face of that kind of longevity, I can't help but think that he and his kind are some of the primary reasons why this city is falling. It occurs to me, though, that Bastian might not see it that way. The world seemed so much different to me just fifteen years ago. What would five hundred years do to a man's perspective?

"What stands out most, in all of your memories?" I ask him, curious in spite of myself.

The prince looks at me strangely, then makes a noise

that's almost a laugh. "You aren't like most tributes, are you? Not like most people, for that matter."

"Is there a difference?" I ask with more heat than I intended. "Between people and tributes?"

His lips quirk and his eyes sparkle with something like amusement. "That's a matter of perspective, I suppose. All chihuahuas are dogs, but not all dogs... you understand." He surveys the city again, then looks at me with renewed interest.

I'm a little worried. This conversation isn't going the way I expected it to at all. Part of me thinks I should just drop the subject, but I bring him back around to the question I asked earlier. Even though I'm not sure I actually want to know his answer, I feel compelled to get inside his head a little, if I can. He's always such an enigma, usually so hard to read, and he's the man who ostensibly runs this place.

"What do you mean when you say I'm not like most people?" I ask, letting the question of tributes vs. people go for the moment.

He flashes me a quick grin. A few days ago, I would have taken it as a threat. Now there's an almost human quality to him. My guard is down, I realize a little belatedly. I don't force it back into place just yet, though. His guard seems to be down a bit as well, and if I clam up, I know he will too.

"Most people—tributes and other vampires—want to

know what powers I've collected. What strength I have. What villages I've conquered, metaphorically and otherwise. You... you ask me about my memories." His voice softens at the end. He sounds gently pensive and a little sad. I catch myself moving closer to him, subconsciously offering him some kind of comfort with my nearness.

For fuck's sake. Comforting vampires? First Connor, now Bastian. If I'm not careful, I'll be comforting Rome next. Or, God forbid, James.

Bastian makes a noise in his throat as he considers my question, drawing my attention back to him. And when he speaks, his answer is nothing like what I expected it would be.

"What I remember most—most vividly and most frequently—is my parents dying," he murmurs. "They were slaughtered in front of my eyes."

He gazes out over the city, but his eyes are haunted, watching a scene I can't see. Remembering every second of their deaths, I'm sure. No matter how long ago it happened, I'm positive he can still recall the exact details.

I take another step toward him in spite of myself. I recognize that look, and the feeling behind it. I know that pain. I *live* in that pain.

"Who killed them?" I ask softly.

"A vampire hunter."

I stare at him, stunned, my heart going still in my chest for a moment as I stop breathing.

We're two sides of the same coin, and only one of us knows it.

For once, Bastian doesn't seem to notice the small shift in my body as I react to his words. He lives in his memory for a moment more, the pain carving deep lines in his young-looking face.

I'm still struggling to breathe right, struggling to push down the emotions surging inside me. I don't know what to do with these feelings. I don't want to get any closer to him, but I can't pull away.

Soon, though, he sighs and smooths his brow, tucking that pain away into some hidden part of himself. All at once, he's Prince Bastian again, royal vampire in need of a tribute.

My heart skips a beat as he moves toward me, closing the small distance between us. There are so many different ways this could go. I feel like I experienced both extremes the day that both James and Rome fed on me, and from what I've seen, Bastian isn't a disgusting animal when he drinks the way James is, but my heart still flutters with nerves.

The prince surprises me again though. Instead of going right for my neck, he turns me around so that I'm facing the city. It glitters and gleams as if it has something to offer, but I know better. Still, the view is killer. So is the man currently putting his arms around me, holding me close, cradling my body against his like a lover.

The worst part is, I have trouble remembering that he's a killer as he brushes the hair off my neck and cradles my head on his shoulder. He doesn't tease—but he doesn't gnaw on me the way James did either. He breathes on my neck just enough to warm it, sending a slow heat spreading through my body.

I barely notice when his teeth slide into me, but I recognize the wave of ecstasy that goes along with the bite. I don't know if it's his practiced touch or his painful confession, but I'm drawn to him. I press close, resting my back against his chest and reaching up to run my fingers through his hair as my other hand holds his larger one flat against my belly.

His lips move on my throat like violent kisses. I can feel his strength, his control… and a bit of leftover melancholy. I understand that. I can't talk about my parents without it fucking up my mood for days. Some part of me hopes I didn't fuck him up by prompting him to recall it, and I tell myself that it's just because a vampire in a shitty mood is more dangerous than a happy one.

I don't entirely believe my own excuse though.

Bastian finishes before I'm ready for the moment to end and licks my wounds closed. He leaves his face where it is, buried in my neck. If I didn't know better, I'd think he was drawing comfort from our embrace.

There's a tug in my soul as we stand on the chilly rooftop together, a dangerous, impulsive urge to throw caution to the wind and open up to him the way he opened up to me.

If I were a different person—if *he* were a different person—I would.

Because the thing I remember most is my parents dying too.

CHAPTER SIXTEEN

"God, it's like high school all over again out there," Jessica complains a few days later as she flops backward onto my bed. "Winona's got a whole clique going. They all hate her. They all worship her. It's gross. Elise is collecting all the short-term girls. She says she's teaching them how to avoid getting picked, but when I asked her to help me learn, she just laughed."

I frown. "She laughed?"

Jessica shrugs miserably, twisting her hair around her finger as she stares at the ceiling. "She says there's nothing she can do for me since I signed such a long-term contract. She says if I had made a point of being able to leave sometime this decade, she could have shown me how to get out of here single, but..."

She trails off, pressing her lips tight together like she's trying not to cry as she runs a hand through her dark hair.

I turn back to the wardrobe, where I'm re-organizing my borrowed clothes for what feels like the hundredth time. Honestly, I don't give a shit about the clothes themselves, or about closet organization, but it gives me something to do with my hands. I get twitchy when I'm anxious, and if I don't find an outlet for the excess energy, it usually comes out in the form of blurting stupid shit at the wrong moment.

"You *are* going to be here for a long time," I point out as gently as I can. "Are you going to try to stay unbonded that whole time, or is there somebody specific you're trying not to bond with?"

Jessica snorts, but I can still hear the tears in her voice. I hang up a shirt and shuffle through the rest of the pile for the matching skirt.

"It's James," she admits thickly. "He's been claiming me every night, and it hurts so bad every single time. Sometimes he forgets to clean up after, and then I have to walk around like a leaky faucet until someone else takes pity on me and closes me up. I can't..." She shakes her head fiercely. "I cannot live with the idea of being bonded to that. Of wanting it in spite of myself. Of seeking out his rough handling."

She sniffles, her voice growing angrier and more panicked with every syllable. "And what then? Vampires don't touch each other's bonded tributes, it's against the bro code or something. Once I'm bonded, that's it. If he leaves me open, he leaves me open, period. No one else will even be able to help me then, and I'll bleed out unless *he* decides to save me."

A hanger snaps in my fist as my jaw clenches so tight my teeth ache.

Motherfucker. I want to kill him. I could go find him right now. It wouldn't be hard. Even the other vampires keep an eye on where he is in order to avoid him—that's how big of a fucking dick he is. Would any of them even care if I shoved a chair leg through his shriveled little heart? No, no they wouldn't. The only thing stopping me is that if I kill one of them, they'll be forced to take me out for the safety of the nest.

But it'd almost be worth it anyway. He's the embodiment of the terror I was expecting when they brought me down here, not to mention the pain. Jessica doesn't deserve that. Nobody does—except maybe Winona—but especially not Jessica. She's here on an angel's errand, dammit.

"It's so fucked up," I growl at the closet. "This whole setup is fucked. They all need to—"

Fuck.

I bite my tongue in the nick of time. Even Jessica doesn't know who I really am or why I'm really here, and I need to keep it that way.

"Need to what?" she asks, her voice muffled by her hands.

I grind my teeth. Nothing fits better than "die," but I can't utter those words, even to my best friend in this place. I take a deep breath, groping around for something to say.

"Remember," I finish blandly. "They need to remember what it's like to be human."

Some of them do. Connor does. Bastian seems to, which surprised the hell out of me, especially given how old he told me he is. Rome feels human—superhuman, even.

Thinking about the three of them acts like fire retardant on my fury, which is frustrating. I can see my mission so clearly when I think about James, but as soon as one of those three pop into my head, everything seems a lot muddier. I can tell myself it's lust or magic or hypnotism or whatever, but the truth is that they just don't feel like thugs or villains. They don't seem very closely related to the vampires I've killed in the street.

"Wouldn't that be nice." Jessica snorts. "But somehow I don't think James was a good person when he was human either. He seems more like the type to spend his mama's tax return on drugs and steal video games from ten-year-olds while beating up on his pregnant teenage girlfriend."

I raise my eyebrows. "Specific," I say mildly.

She shrugs, looking sheepish. "He reminds me of my cousin's ex-boyfriend. Like, a lot."

"Gross."

"Right?" She shakes her head and sighs. "You think if I pretend I'm sick, I won't have to go to dinner?"

I shake my head. "I think if you pretend you're sick, they'll get a doctor in here and make sure you aren't infecting the rest of the herd."

She makes a face. "You're probably right. Ugh." She shudders and goes quiet for a while, chewing on her lip. Then she glances at me again, her large eyes sad. "Did you ever think you would end up like this? Corralled like a cow, competing to see who's going to be sticking their fork in your flank for the rest of your life?"

I shake my head. "Never crossed my mind until it happened."

"You know the worst part?" she asks, her voice very quiet.

"What?"

Tears fill her eyes. She looks—ashamed? That can't be right. She has nothing to be ashamed of.

Jessica swallows hard and moistens her lips. "It's already starting," she murmurs. "The more he feeds on me, the less I hate it. It hurts like a bitch every single time, but at least I know it's going to be over soon. When he takes a while to get to me, I find myself looking for him. I don't want that. I never wanted to be that girl."

Fat tears roll down her cheeks, and my chest constricts. I cross over to the bed, sitting down and wrapping an arm around her shoulders.

"Hey, it's not you," I tell her earnestly. "It's something about the bite. I don't know why James's bites don't come with that endorphin rush—I think it's because he attacks rather than kisses—but still, there's some kind of magic that goes into it. They *want* you to get attached, Jess. It's not your fault that a magic older than civilization works on you. It's just evolution."

I don't know if any of that is true, honestly. It could just be Stockholm Syndrome for all I know. If it is, I've got it too.

"It's affecting me too," I say to her. "I can't get through the salad course without looking for Connor or Rome or Bastian."

She snorts and pulls away from me, giving me a look. "If you were anybody else, I'd accuse you of humble bragging."

I grin. "Hell, if *you* were anybody else, you'd be accusing me of humble bragging. If I was looking for other friends here, I'd be shit outta luck."

She laughs, but the sound trails into a sympathetic noise, because it's true. My getting consistent attention from those three has not endeared me to anybody—least of all Winona, who is just as focused on ruling over the other tributes as she is on snagging a member of the vampire court. I've never met anyone as power hungry as she is.

"Well, at least none of them are brutal," she says with a sigh. "Not to the tributes, anyway. James is a monster."

"Yeah." I nod, anger rushing through me again. I don't let it show on my face though, giving her a sympathetic smile. "Hey—how about a headache to get out of dinner?"

In the end, she decides to try for a migraine. There's nothing infectious about those, and girls seem to come down with them a lot. Probably something to do with losing blood all the damn time, but I'm not a doctor.

Anastasyia lets her stay in bed and promises to cover for her if anyone asks about her. The vampire matron is actually one of the few people here who treats us as more than meat. She's a lot kinder than I would've expected. I sort of want to know her story, but I also know that I need to *stop* learning more about the people I'm running away from. I can already feel the hangover from the amount of whiskey I'll need to drown out the survivor's guilt.

Speaking of survivors, the male tributes are on time for dinner for once. As usual, I sneak a quick glance at my brother to check in on him as we all file into the great hall, and my brows furrow when I catch sight of him.

Nathan is trailing behind the group by several yards. Every movement is stiff and slow, as if he aged fifty years since I last saw him. It reminds me of the time he got his ass kicked by a bunch of teenage BloodGods—he never did tell me why, but it's not a huge mystery. A bigger mystery is why he's walking around looking like that now, when he's supposed to be under the vampires' dubious protection.

I'm at the back of the group of female tributes too, so it isn't hard to drift back a little farther to intercept Nathan. He doesn't even seem to see me until I touch his wrist, then he jumps like he's been shocked.

"Hey. What's the matter with you?" I ask, keeping my voice low.

He inhales sharply, hissing through his teeth. He's pale, skinnier than he was last week, his eyes dull over dark circles. He's still shaking, even though he clearly knows it's me now. A sharp twist of worry sets all of my senses on edge. Dammit, I should have been keeping a closer eye on him. The little check-ins I try to do clearly haven't been enough.

"It's... it's Althea and Maureen," he says, his voice a dry, harsh whisper. "They've got a pissing contest going. I'm the prize."

He gives me a wan smile, showing me his sunken, withdrawn gum line. My stomach bottoms out. Fucking hell. They're sucking the life out of him.

"Show me who they are," I growl. "I'll kill them right now. Fuck this."

I start for the door, but Nathan grabs me before I can go more than two steps. Even his grasp is weak, dammit. "Mikka, stop. You can't kill them, the rest of them will eat you alive. You know that. You have a plan, remember? Play the long game. Attacking now is stupid. You're not stupid."

I whirl around, narrowing my eyes at him. "I'm not

going to just sit here and let them kill you by inches, Nathan."

"Then don't." He shrugs tiredly. All the fight has gone out of him just like that, and the sight of his listless expression makes rage boil in my veins. "But don't be stupid. Okay?"

I don't want to agree, but if we stay out whispering in the corridor any longer, someone's going to come looking for us.

"Okay," I say flatly. "But you better *promise* to come straight to me if you need help. You hear me?"

"Yeah, I hear you, Mimi," he murmurs, a little smile tugging at the corner of his mouth. "I promise."

"Good."

"Now—dinner time." He gives me a firm look, then walks away from me, shuffling like an old man.

Fire crackles in my soul, but I follow him into the dining room.

I don't know what I'll do if I see those two bitches crawling over him tonight. The fury churning inside me doesn't care much about subtle plans.

CHAPTER SEVENTEEN

I can't eat. I can't even pretend to eat.

All of my attention is on Nathan, who's shoveling food into his mouth as fast as possible. I know why—the female vampires aren't exactly hiding their intentions. I see them eyeing one another from across the room, one on either side of Nathan. One's a tall blonde, her trim figure built out like a tennis player. The other one is a few inches shorter, round at hip and breast, an olive-skinned girl with dark curls down to her ass and long purple nails filed into points.

They barely let him finish his first course before they start surreptitiously moving toward him. They act like they're mingling, play at being distracted by conversation, but every move they make is toward Nathan. The brunette gets to him first, petting him with those long nails absently while she carries on a conversation with another vampire.

Nathan tenses, then slowly relaxes as she keeps petting him. She's just marking her territory—for now. I glance around, looking for the blonde. She's watching Nathan too, her eyes slitted with territorial fury as she moves closer to him. The brunette sees her and grins, then tips Nathan's chin up to kiss her. He does, but I see his shoulders go rigid again. He knows what's coming.

A second later, it happens. The brunette bites him, drinking deeply. *Too* deeply. Rather than embrace her, as most tributes find themselves doing when bitten by a skilled vamp, his hands just go limp. Rage stiffens my spine. The blonde is moving like a jungle cat now, stalking him from across the room, waiting for her moment.

"Would you care to dance, my lady?"

Connor's voice barely breaks through my focus, and I jerk my head up to look at him. His crooked smile and sunshine eyes don't have the calming effect on me they usually do. Nothing could unwind the knot of tension in my gut right now.

I want to wave him off impatiently so I can keep watching Nathan, but I'm pretty sure that wouldn't go over well. Even if he doesn't take offense to it—which, knowing Connor, he probably wouldn't—I know other vampires are waiting for their chance to get to me. So I lift my hand for him, meeting his eyes briefly. I think I smile at him, but honestly, I'm not sure.

We move to the dance floor. He's chatting away about

something as usual in his deep, warm voice, but I'm not paying attention. I make the right noises at the right places, I think, but I have no idea what he's talking about. Not a single word makes it past my inner ear.

The brunette vampiress finishes and keeps a possessive hand on Nathan's shoulder. I'm sure all of the attention would be flattering, if she wasn't about to kill him. Nathan looks miserable. He shouldn't look so unhappy right after being fed from. If she was pouring sensuality into her kiss, it should have triggered that feeling of ecstasy that I'm way too familiar with by now—but if he's too drained, maybe it doesn't matter. Blood magic doesn't work without blood.

The brunette waves at someone across the room. As soon as her hand is off Nathan, the blonde is on his lap. Jesus, she's fast. I didn't even see her move. She takes the other side of his neck. There's a gray hue to his skin now, and a damp sheen across his forehead.

"Hey." Connor's voice is gentle, and it breaks through the rushing sound that fills my ears. "You've stepped on my foot like four times."

"Sorry," I mutter.

Dammit, where did the brunette go?

There she is, not more than a dozen steps away from Nathan. She's glaring at the blonde, but her mouth is smiling as she chatters away with whoever she's talking to. Is she going to go back in again once blondie finishes up? They really will fucking kill him.

"Oh it's fine, nothing an amputation won't fix."

"Good," I say absently.

The blonde has stopped, but I still can't breathe. She's grinning over my brother's shoulder at the brunette. Nathan's forehead is on her shoulder, but I don't think it's a sexual gesture. His whole posture is limp. He might just not have the strength to raise his head.

"Yes, it is good. I've always wanted a prosthetic. I'm thinking a flamingo foot. Or a peg leg, like a pirate, as long as I can paint it pink. What do you think?"

"Mm-hm, sounds good."

Dammit, the brunette is working her way back. If she feeds from him again, he's not going to walk out of here. Doesn't anybody pay attention to these things? Aren't there rules for overfeeding? There should be, but somehow, I'm not surprised that there aren't.

"Okay, that's it." Connor pulls me to a stop in the middle of the dance floor. I crane my neck to keep looking toward Nathan, but he touches my face, pulling my gaze to him. "What's wrong?"

I blink at him a few times, but my mind is blank. I don't know what to say, or how to play off my obvious distress and distraction. Would he even care that a male tribute is in danger? Would he get jealous?

No, Connor isn't the person to talk to about this. It's not that I don't think he would care, since he's one of the most empathetic people I've ever met. But he's too new and too *nice*. No one will listen to him. He doesn't have enough power in the vampire hierarchy yet.

"I need a second," I tell him. "I'm sorry."

"It's okay," he murmurs, but his brow is furrowed with worry. I kiss his cheek and leave him on the dance floor.

He doesn't follow me, but I can feel his eyes on me. I'm breaking a whole lot of psycho-social rules right now, and I know it, but I can't just sit here and do nothing. I scan the great hall, chewing on my bottom lip as my heart races.

Rome isn't hard to find. As usual, he's standing to one side of the large room, watching vampires go about their business with stern eyes.

Blood tributes aren't really supposed to approach vampires uninvited. I've seen girls get slapped, scolded, and snubbed for doing just that. The snubbing was the worst, from a social hierarchy perspective. Girls who were snubbed didn't get chosen again, by anybody, for days at least.

But this is Rome. From everything I've seen, he's not exactly a stickler for those kinds of rules.

He sees me coming and focuses on me, eyes and body attuning to me. He's studying my face and opening his tense posture, his body language an invitation, so I keep walking toward him, praying that I'm right and that he won't shoot me down for approaching him uninvited.

"Can we speak privately?" I ask quietly as I come within earshot.

He nods and offers me his elbow. It's a more natural movement for him than it is for Connor, which makes me wonder, briefly, just how old Rome is. I don't bother asking though. It's not what's important right now.

As soon as we're out in the corridor, I let go of his arm and turn to face him. "Did you mean it when you told me I should come to you if there are any vampires being abusive?"

He tenses, his eyes flashing with murderous intent. "Who hurt you?"

I shake my head. "Not me. It's a couple of others. Nathan—that tall, skinny tribute with the prison tattoos down his left side—is being drunk from too often. Althea and Maureen are draining him dry fighting over him. He's not going to last another day if they don't back off. And Jessica... you've met her, right?"

"I have."

"She's James's favorite, and he's not being careful with her. When he's done with her, he leaves her to bleed until she can find someone else to put her back together. If he chooses her to bond with, he'll kill her."

Rome's expression is closed-off, unreadable. He's not the most expressive vampire in the world to begin with, but there's some kind of tension behind his eyes that I can't figure out. I need him to hear me, but I don't know what to say that I haven't already said. Does he need to be convinced that they're worth it?

I open my mouth to speak, but he speaks first.

"Why do you care so much about the others?" he asks, his voice tight.

I didn't expect that question, and can't quite mitigate my reaction. "What? Because... because they're people! They're my fellow tributes. Fellow humans. I'd do the same for any of them."

Even Winona, although it pains me a little to admit it to myself.

Rome's expression softens. I'm not sure how he was expecting me to answer that question, but his response to the answer I gave surprises me.

He cups my face in his hand, running a thumb over my lip. His warm eyes linger on my mouth for a moment, just long enough to make me suck in a surprised breath, and then he leans in and presses his lips to mine.

His kiss is startlingly human.

It's not a demand, not a precursor to a bite—just a kiss.

Relief washes through me, and I kiss him back. I can't help it. I'm glad I came to him, and I'm certain now that I made the right choice. He's solid and warm, a force to be reckoned with. I can feel the killer under the surface, but I know it isn't me he wants to hurt. I'm safe here, in his arms, at least for the moment.

After a long moment, he pulls away just enough to look into my eyes. The blue and violet of his dark irises seem to swirl, as if entire galaxies are contained within his eyes. He brushes my hair back away from my face, then releases me entirely.

As I watch, the softness and warmth in his face disappears under a veneer of hard-edged ruthlessness. It sends shivers down my spine. Not fear, but something similar.

"I'll take care of it," he tells me.

There isn't a single part of me that doubts his words.

CHAPTER EIGHTEEN

"You look better," I tell Jessica, who's perched on the edge of my bed. There's a little smile playing around her eyes, an expression I haven't seen on her before.

"*So* much better." She shakes her head, letting out a happy sigh. "I don't know what happened, but after I had that migraine"—she puts air quotes around the word —"James backed off. He doesn't seem to have a new favorite either. He's sort of just bouncing around, picking up a new girl here or there. Without him hovering over me all the time, I've met some new vampires. A couple of them... I dunno. I actually wouldn't mind if they choose me on Saturday."

My stomach ties itself into a tight knot at the reminder of my rapidly dwindling window in which to escape with Nathan. Saturday is just five days from now, and I still don't have as clear of an exit strategy as I'd like. Although

I've managed to get a glimpse of the keypad on the sleek glass elevator Bastian took me up in, I don't have the complete code yet.

And I'm running out of time.

Jessica doesn't notice my mood shift at all, continuing on blithely. "There are three interested in me now, and they're all pretty gentle. There's George, Xavier, and..." She pauses for a moment, smiling shyly. "And Violet."

I grin at her, shoving my anxiety down. "Violet, huh?"

She nods, her eyes sparkling. "I never thought I could feel things like that for a woman. People seem pretty straight around here. Traditional, you know? She's keeping it on the down-low, but she comes to me more than the other two do—and I like it. I like her."

I wouldn't have believed a tribute could truly like a vampire just a few weeks ago, but now I understand. I like a few of them myself. Specifically, Rome and Connor. Bastian loses points for being the figurehead. If he wasn't at the top of the food chain, maybe I'd like him too.

Smiling at Jessica, I nudge her with my elbow. "I'm happy for you."

It's the truth. I'm not as worried about her now, though I still hate the thought of leaving her behind. I'm running out of time to get me and Nathan out, and I certainly don't have time to convince Jessica to leave with us, especially with her mother's life on the line. She's not selfish enough to make it an easy argument.

But regardless of who I end up taking with me, I need to be as prepared as possible for the escape attempt.

Later that night, after everyone's in their rooms, I pull my weapons out. I haven't been practicing like I should have been, too caught up in survival and navigating the social web to focus on training. It was a stupid oversight on my part, but worth it. Jessica isn't the only one who's been having a better time of it since my talk with Rome. Now that Nathan's not being sucked dry every night by Althea and Maureen, I'm confident that he'll be strong enough to leave with me when the time comes.

I'm stiff and awkward for a minute or two as I go through the warm-ups, but my muscles quickly remember what they're doing. All the tension I've built up over the last several days flows out through my hands, into my weapons, focusing my movements. I work up a good sweat, running all my favorite drills before I tuck the weapons back in their hiding place and crawling into bed.

I stare up at the ceiling as I wait for my heart rate to slow down and for sleep to come. I almost have the keypad figured out. That means I almost have the key to getting out of this place.

From now on, that has to be my main focus.

I have to figure out that code.

The next day, I head back toward the elevator that Bastian and I rode in as soon as I finish breakfast.

I know the first three digits and the last digit. I'm only missing two now, and I'm out of time to play it subtle. No matter what it takes, I need to finish up today. As soon as that happens, I'll go find Nathan and get us the hell out of here. This elevator is the only viable escape option I've found, so no matter what, we have to make it work.

I'm approaching the intersection, my "dazed tribute" face going full force. I can hear someone coming from the elevator, so I lay it on extra thick, stumbling over my own toes just a little. The vampire rounds the corner, and—

Fuck.

It's Connor.

I wipe the stupid look off my face, but I'm not quick enough. His bright smile fades slightly as worry rises around his eyes.

"Darcy! What are you doing here? Are you okay?"

"Oh, yes, I'm fine," I say, trying to wave it off. "I was just, um, trying to find my way back."

There's a flash of jealousy, or maybe protectiveness, in his expression. It gives me a warm feeling deep down inside that I can't afford to pay much attention to. Every time I see him, every time I talk to him, it's always a fight to remind myself of what he is.

He offers me his arm and a wide smile.

"Well, m'lady," he says theatrically. "Allow me to

escort you back to the tribute wing. Er—if that's where you want to go."

I could ask him to take me up in the elevator, but I'm worried about other vamps seeing us. I get the feeling that Bastian taking me to the top floor was something he doesn't do with most tributes. In fact, I'm not sure he's *ever* done it before, and I'm pretty sure if he finds out I was asking Connor to take me up, it'll either piss him off or make him suspicious. So instead of mentioning it, I play dumb, hating myself for using Connor like this.

Doesn't matter. He's a fucking vampire, Mikka.

"What's through there?" I ask, nodding toward the elevator he just got off of.

"Ugh, just boring offices and stuff. Nobody ever told me that vampires had to work for an undeadening." He rolls his eyes, and it makes me grin in spite of myself.

"An undeadening, huh?"

"Well it can't really be called a living, can it?" He grins, winking at me. "Even though you *have* managed to inject a lot more life into this stuffy old tomb."

"Me?" Huh. That's exactly the opposite of what I want to do.

"Sure! What other gorgeous tribute would have put up with my clumsy ass this whole time?"

"Plenty," I tell him. Seriously, he has no idea how many of the girls hate me for being on easy terms with him.

He throws back his head and laughs. "You're biased,"

he teases. "And cool. Super cool, like—" He breaks off, groping around for words.

"Ice cold?" I offer helpfully.

He laughs again. It's like music and feels like a concert at the inner harbor on a warm summer evening. Dammit, why does he have to be a vampire?

"See? Right there. You're cooler than cool. Most of the other girls I've talked to since getting here have a very specific idea of what they're in for, and most of them find it, or something close to it. They want a brooding perpetual teen who owns stock in body glitter, or a dramatic middle-aged gentleman whose closet is full of tuxedos."

"I have seen plenty of both," I agree. "Though I gotta say, there are more brutes than I'd anticipated."

That's a lie. If anything, I thought there would be more vicious animals, but I think it fits with his general perception of tribute expectations.

"James and Chris." Connor nods with a wince. "Yeah, they're not really royal court material. I mean, I'm not either, but not for lack of trying. They used to live on the surface, and they liked it." He shudders. "I don't know about you, but basement apartments in abandoned buildings don't sound like a lot of fun to me."

"Sounds pretty awful," I agree. "But way more suited to their personalities. James's, anyway. I don't think I've met Chris."

"Good," he says firmly. "I hope you never do."

"So why do they live here now?"

He shrugs. "I don't know the specifics, but I guess there's some kind of Buffy wannabe running around up there causing trouble. They claim they only came down here because they felt they deserved better, but I'm pretty sure they're just scared."

Don't smile, don't smile.

I focus on the "Buffy wannabe" statement and let it annoy me enough to keep from grinning like an idiot. Apparently, I had James on the run once, and dammit, I'll do it again.

Connor smiles down at me, his eyes warm and soft, and moves his arm so that my hand slides into his. He kisses my wrist, then lets our hands swing between us. It's cozy, comfortable... and exactly what I don't need right now.

Shit. It's going to hurt to leave him.

I shove the knowledge away, wishing I could make it untrue just by ignoring it. If I get melancholy right now, he'll know something's up, and he won't stop pestering me until he finds out what it is. Because he cares.

Dammit, Connor, act like a vampire for once, would you?

His pocket buzzes when we reach the main staircase. I wonder if the stairs go up to the building above too, or if they just reach into higher underground levels? I'm about to ask him, but he's frowning at his phone.

"What's wrong?" I ask.

He sighs, taps out a text, and slides the phone back into his pocket. "One of the older vampires was trying to enter data onto a spreadsheet I've been keeping for some of our accounting stuff, and he managed to mess up what was already there. At least he thinks he messed it up. He probably just hit 'show formulas' or something, but I have to go fix it regardless."

I raise an eyebrow. "Older, like—?"

He grins. "Older like rotary phones are newfangled technology and why in heaven's name don't we keep proper pens around here anymore, haven't you any idea how wasteful these 'point balls' are?"

He scowls like an old man, making his voice gruff and grumpy until he can't hold in his laughter any longer.

I laugh along with him, and he pulls me close, holding me securely against his chest. I bury my face in his shirt and wrap my arms around his waist, relishing the warmth of him all around me. I breathe him in, memorizing the way he feels and sounds, memorizing the way I feel when I'm with him. I'll need these memories to keep me sane after I leave.

On the other hand, maybe holding on to these feelings is what will eventually drive me crazy—or get me killed. Because I'm not going to stop hunting vampires, and I can't afford to show restraint on the street. Knowing that some of the monsters I kill might laugh like music and smell like warm rain in their home element will leave me with a guilt that whiskey won't be able to touch.

He pulls away from me and kisses my forehead, then my nose, then my mouth. He lingers there a while until his phone buzzes again. Then he pulls away, eyes full of regret, and brushes his fingers over my face.

"Ah, parting is such sweet sorrow," he sighs.

I grin. "I didn't think you were a Shakespeare kind of guy."

His brow furrows. "Shakespeare? I thought that was Willy Wonka!"

I can't tell if he's serious or not, but he's gone before I stop laughing. I watch his cocky little strut as he disappears back the way we came from. For an instant, I consider following him, just because I know that he's going to have to punch the code in to get upstairs, but I reject the idea as soon as it occurs to me. He's too aware of my presence. Accepting momentary defeat, I head back to my room. Once I'm sure that Connor has moved on, I sneak out again and spend the rest of the day hanging out near the corridor where the elevator sits, but I don't have any luck.

At dinner, every bite of food seems to go down my throat like a lump of cement, and I even go as far as veering out of the way instead of heading straight back to my room after the feast is finally over. But there are no vampires using the elevator at this time of "night," since it's actually late morning topside, so there's nothing to see. I'm tempted to punch in what I know and guess the rest, but I don't want to risk setting off an alarm with too many wrong guesses.

Disgruntled and on-edge, I head back to the tribute wing.

The moment I open the door to my little bedroom, I know something is wrong.

I can *feel* it even before I take in the chaotic mess that's strewn about the space, like something hovering in the air. My mattress is lying cockeyed, contorted at an angle from the bedframe to the floor. Sheets and blankets lie scattered over the stone floor, along with all of my clothes and shoes.

Motherfucker.

My room has been ransacked.

CHAPTER NINETEEN

Fuck. What the hell happened in here?

Fear clouds my brain, but a rush of adrenaline parts the clouds in my mind. Someone found out. Someone must have suspected me for some reason. Maybe because I went to Rome and tattled on the other vampires? Or did someone notice that I always seem to be out wandering, and that I tend to stick to certain parts of the palace on my meandering walks?

I want to punch a wall. Better yet, a vampire.

I have to get to Nathan, have to get us out of here before one or both of us gets killed. Did they find my weapons? If they did, I'll be lucky to get ten feet, never mind trying to get across the palace to the men's wing.

My mouth is dry, but my heart has finally come down out of my ears to rattle my ribcage at a more reasonable volume.

As my hearing returns to normal, something catches my attention out in the hallway. A whispered voice, quiet but high-pitched.

"—would have paid to see her face!"

"God, I would pay my whole bid price for a spy cam right now."

Tittering laughter follows that statement, and my hands curl into fists. Something that's part relief, part anger, and part annoyance rises up from my belly in a wave as I realize it wasn't a vampire who went through my room.

It was a human. *Several* humans.

Several petty fucking bitches.

Fury, eager to be tapped after such a long suppression, overwhelms my lingering panic in an instant, and I move, spinning away from my open door. Here I am, trying to save my damn brother, and these assholes are pulling middle school fucking pranks. Blind rage fills every taut fiber of my being as I stalk the sounds to their source.

The girls are huddled in Winona's room, whispering and giggling.

Several of them yelp as I crash into the room, but I'm not interested. Winona is sitting smugly on her bed, posing like some debutante princess. She gives me a cool, bored look.

Yeah? We'll see how bored you are in a second, you twat.

She's expecting a verbal altercation, so I don't give it to

her. Instead, I grab her by her hair and slam her into the wall.

The girls all scream in unison as my fist connects with Winona's perfectly symmetrical face hard enough to make blood spray from her nose. Winona stares in shock, tense but frozen, her pupils like tiny, terrified islands in the middle of wide white pools. I let go of her, and she slides to the floor, her eyes never leaving me.

"You stupid, petty *children*," I growl. "Is this why you came here? Is this why you sold your life away to bloodsuckers? Just so you could live out some mean girl fantasy? You idiots! *You*." I point at Winona, who cringes away from me. "You have done nothing but drive wedges between tributes since the moment you set your porcelain feet in the palace. Are you out of your mind? The only people you have on your side are the other tributes! Everybody else either wants to eat you or get you paired up with a vampire A.S.A motherfucking P. so they can get your dramatic bullshit out of their workplace!"

Winona's jaw stiffens and she looks away.

"Yeah, that's what I thought," I grit out between my teeth. Then I turn to the girls on the bed. "And the rest of you, you're really just going to follow her and do whatever she says? Why? She'd sell each and every one of you out just as fast as she sold herself, and you know it."

They gave each other shifty looks, with more than a few sending wary glares in Winona's direction.

"Now." I'm still shaking with fury, trying to bottle it back up before I do any permanent damage either to the girls or to my "willing tribute" reputation, but it's like a dam has broken inside me. "Now," I say again. "Don't touch my shit. Don't go in my room. And leave me the fuck alone."

I stalk away, leaving a stunned, suspicious silence behind me. If I'm lucky, their little clique will tear itself apart from the inside out before dawn.

Or maybe not. Hitting Winona—while it felt fantastic and was definitely deserved—might have made her a mean girl martyr.

Yup, there it is.

I'm barely back to my room and already I can hear a couple of the girls making sympathetic noises in Winona's direction.

Maybe the broken nose will give her face character. Or hell, maybe it'll give *her* character.

A second look at my room keeps my adrenaline up. I'm hot and loose and ready for war. If the assholes who fucked up my room weren't so soft and pampered, maybe I could have worked some of this off with a good fight. But they aren't the types to jump a bitch, oh no. They're the types to dump a bucket of pig's blood all over her and sit behind innocent eyes and wicked smiles while the world around them devolves into chaos.

The real question is, how far did they actually go? Did

they find anything that matters? The *only* thing that matters?

Ignoring the clothes and bedding on the floor, I stalk to the wardrobe and pry open the drawer at the bottom. They knocked it off its runners, so it takes me a minute to get it open—a very loud, very long minute full of very unladylike words. But eventually, it gives way, sliding out.

The dress I wore to begin this charade is still sitting on top, exactly how I left it. That doesn't mean anything though—if they have even one functional brain between them, they wouldn't want to make it obvious that they saw the weapons. If they did, that is.

The dress gets stuck as I pull on it, and I've got several more choice words for that. I put my back into it and almost fall over when the drawer finally gives it up, but I catch myself and throw the dress to one side instead. The gleam of cool steel in the drawer doesn't give me much relief, I'm too wound up, but I pull them out anyway. I need to feel the steel in my hands.

I pull my twin blades out and grip the handles so tightly that my knuckles turn white. I stand quickly, whirling around to look for another hiding place now that the drawer's been compromised—and freeze when I realize I'm not alone.

Rome stands just inside the doorway to my room, the heavy wood closed behind him.

I didn't even hear him coming. I didn't hear him open it or close it.

Shit.

I freeze. He's frozen too, his eyes wide with shock, his mouth slightly agape as our eyes lock. Cold focus channels my adrenaline, my fighting instincts overriding everything else.

He saw me. He knows too much. I can't let him live.

The second he closes his mouth, I move. But so does he. I jump, crossing the blades in front of me, targeting his throat. His strong, muscular throat. The throat that spoke up for Nathan and Jessica, even though his only connection to them was me. The throat I've kissed. The neck I've clung to.

I slide the blades open a fraction of a second too soon, land clumsily—and get snagged.

His strong hands are vices around my wrists. He lifts me, pulling me in one smooth motion until my weight is only barely on my feet, until I struggle to breathe. With a sudden jerk and twist, he forces the blades out of my hands, letting them clang to the floor.

"I should kill you," he growls, his voice low and harsh.

My heart slams in my chest at the sound of those words coming from his lips. There are plenty of vamps I expected might try to murder me in this place, but Rome has never been one of them.

Until now.

"It's my *duty* to kill you," he repeats. There's more force behind the words now.

"Who are you trying to convince, Rome? Me, or yourself?" The words hiss out painfully. There's not enough air in my chest to propel them properly.

His eyes narrow. In a single, smooth movement, almost faster than I can make sense of, he slams my wrists down to my sides, spins me around, and holds me tight against him with one arm. His other hand grabs my hair in a knot on the back of my head, forcing me to bend over and look at my blades. My ass is pressed hard against his hips, and the strange intimacy of our position only makes my pulse throb harder in my veins.

"Tell me where you got those."

"Pawn shop," I lie through clenched teeth.

His grip tightens painfully against me and he twists his wrist, pulling my hair until I have to bite back a yelp.

"Pawn shops don't keep blessed slayer weapons in stock," he growls. "Not around here. They know better."

I laugh weakly. "You're assuming a lot of brains for people who look at the world and decide that their life's mission is to run an overpriced junkyard and loan."

He spins me out of his arms hard enough to slam me against the wall. I tuck my head forward and my arms back —you only get knocked out like this once before you learn how to avoid it. But it almost doesn't matter. I hit the wall hard enough to nearly crack my tailbone, and the shock of it freezes my legs for a second.

"You're a spy," Rome growls as he takes two long steps across the room. "Betrayer."

I make the mistake of looking up into his eyes. If he was only furious, maybe I would be able to ignore the shadow of guilt lurking around the edges of my fear. But there's something else in his eyes, something that forces the guilt out of hiding, solidifying it. He's *hurt*. I hurt him, after he's been kind to me, after he put himself in harm's way to protect me and my fellow tributes.

I drop my head, forcing my gaze away from his eyes as I shove down the shame and regret that try to rise up inside me.

It doesn't matter. The only good vampire is a dead vampire.

Maybe they can't help what they are, but neither can I—and I'm not about to die at the hands of a vampire, no matter how kind he can be. Especially not with Nathan still in danger.

Rome reaches out for my head, and I drop my shoulders and charge. Thankfully, the dress I chose for dinner tonight has a flowy, loose-fitting skirt, so it doesn't impede my movements. He's top-heavy, his broad chest and shoulders outweighing his hips and legs, and he topples under the force of my tackle.

He knows how to fight though.

He rolls with the fall, flinging me over his head as he somersaults backwards, landing on his feet while I'm still skidding across the floor.

I scramble for a blade, and he kicks it out of reach, trying to stomp on my fingers with his other foot. I leap out of the way, then swing my legs around, catching his ankles hard.

He stumbles, and I don't let the opening go to waste. I hit his chin as it comes down, knocking him back, but it barely fazes him. He catches my leg and yanks me off the ground so I'm dangling with my head level to his crotch, my skirt dangling down around my arms and face.

With a feral snarl, I jab at him—even vampire men are vulnerable to nut shots—but he twists, making my fist connect with his hip.

I kick with my free leg instead and catch him in the temple hard enough for him to reflexively drop me. I hit the ground on my hands and toes, ready to move, but he slams down on top of me like a wrestler.

He outweighs me by a lot, and I flatten beneath him, but he moves his arms—probably reaching to snap my neck—and that gives me enough space to flip onto my back beneath him and strike for his face.

Rome jerks up out of the way, avoiding my punch by less than an inch. His large frame settles between my hips, his weight bearing down on me and pressing me into the floor. I jab again, and he catches my hand, pinning it to the floor above my head. In the same move, he pins my other wrist. His eyes blaze mere inches from mine. His entire body is covering mine now, all the way from my wrists to my hips.

My breath rattles in my chest, my throat so tight I can barely suck in enough oxygen.

He has me, and we both know it. A headbutt and a quick twist of my neck, and I'll be finished. That's all it will take, and I can't figure a way to avoid it.

But he doesn't move.

I meet his eyes again, still breathing hard. He's conflicted, I can see it. It's the same conflict that made me hesitate to take his head off. My heart rate ratchets up a couple notches, but it's not from fear, although I wish it was. I can feel heat building in his groin, which is pressed hard against me. My body—betrayer, indeed—is reacting. He inhales sharply and his eyes darken. He knows. He can probably smell it on me with his enhanced senses.

Silence deepens around us, heavy with meaning, vibrating with indecision. The longer I gaze into his eyes, the deeper the silence gets.

My breath steadies as I draw his scent into my nostrils. Maybe it *is* Stockholm syndrome. Maybe it's just the way he's looking at me right now, like he wishes he'd caught me doing literally anything else. Like he cares about me enough that I actually have the power to hurt him.

Whatever it is, I can't break our gaze.

When he does move, it's slow and uncertain. Rather than his forehead connecting with mine in the headbutt I was expecting, it's his lips that press against my own, soft and warm... and angry. It's a different kind of anger, a specific kind, like when I'm reaming Nathan for being stupid and putting his life in danger.

Arching beneath his large body, I kiss Rome back, throwing everything I have into it.

It's not quite an apology, not quite an explanation—just an acceptance of his anger.

And of my own.

CHAPTER TWENTY

Rome's lips are bruising, and I can feel the scrape of his teeth against my tongue as our mouths open, gasps and grunts pouring back and forth between us as the kiss deepens. He tastes good, so fucking good, like warm mulled wine and the richest kind of chocolate—with just a hint of the coppery tang of blood.

As he devours me with his mouth and I do my best to consume him right back, I realize how badly some part of me has wanted to do this ever since that first time he drank from me. The way he prepared my neck and then finally bit into it was careful and almost tender, everything about it measured and controlled.

But this?

This is the opposite.

The other side of the coin.

This is Rome when he's not holding himself back,

when he's letting both his sensual gentleness and his rage run free.

It's addictive and terrifying all at once, and I lose myself in the weight of his lips and the heat of his breath until he suddenly pulls back, breaking the connection between us.

I let out a quiet, strangled cry of disappointment, my head lifting from the stone floor as I chase his mouth. But he wraps a hand around my throat and squeezes just hard enough to keep me pinned down, his dark blue eyes meeting mine. The look entirely black in this light, like staring up at a night sky when it's so overcast you can't see a single star.

My eyelids flutter as I gaze up at him, my chest rising and falling as I suck in a breath past the pressure of his hand. His fingers are long and calloused, and his palm is so broad that it covers my entire throat. I know he can feel my pulse fluttering wildly against his skin, and his nostrils flare as his jaw muscles ripple.

For a moment, I wonder if he'll snap my neck. He wouldn't even have to twist my head to kill me—he could crush my windpipe and the bones of my spine all in one vicious squeeze if he chose to do it.

Maybe he's thinking about it.

Maybe that's what's going on behind those midnight-blue eyes of his.

I can't tell what internal battle he's fighting with himself. I only know when it ends.

With a low snarl, he releases my throat and drops his head again, kissing me even more savagely than the first time, as if he's trying to punish me or himself or both of us. I barely have time to return the kiss before he's ripping his lips away from mine again, but this time, he doesn't draw back. He just drags them downward, over my jawline and chin and down the column of my throat.

His sharp fangs tease the throbbing pulse of my carotid artery, making bolts of sensation charge through my body, but he doesn't bite down. He moves lower, his ravenous mouth laying waste to the lines of my collarbones, making my nipples peak in response. Then he's moving lower still, his large hands grabbing fistfuls of my twisted, torn skirt and shoving it upward until he's kneeling between my legs with nothing but my panties between him and my core.

My pussy clenches hard as his hot breath ghosts over my skin, and I jerk in shock as he shreds the delicate lace of my underwear with a quick slash of his teeth. One hand yanks the destroyed fabric away, tossing it to the side as he buries his face between my legs.

Just like the way he kissed me, there's something brutal and unrestrained about it, not a single thing held back. I'm already wet as fuck from having his tongue in my mouth and his lips and teeth all over my neck, and instead of just licking me, he smells me, dragging his nose through my folds and nudging it against my clit in a way that makes me whimper.

"You smell just as good as I remember," he murmurs roughly, and I blink up at the ceiling in confusion.

When...?

Oh. When he drank from me. I was so turned on then that even without his face buried between my legs, he could smell my arousal.

My breath comes faster, and I rock my hips against the cool, hard floor, seeking out more pressure and friction right where I need it.

Rome's nose brushes my clit again, and his tongue delves inside me briefly, but then he pulls back. I'm whimpering, almost mindless with the need to feel him again, and when he puts his mouth on me again, I gasp.

Because it's not where I expected it.

Instead of licking my pussy, his tongue drags up the inside of my thigh. I bite my lip at the agonizing tease, goosebumps spreading out over my skin. He laps at me again, but this time I feel the drag of teeth too, and that's even better. Even closer to the thing I didn't even know I needed until now.

"Rome," I pant, clenching my hands into fists to keep myself from reaching down and shoving his face against my leg. Some part of me still can't admit I like this so much, or that I need it so badly. "Fuck..."

He doesn't give me what I want, and he doesn't pay any attention to my words. He just keeps teasing me, warming me up with his tongue and his breath before pulling away enough to let the air cool my heated skin. He switches to my other leg, his teeth scraping against the tender flesh of my inner thigh, and my clit throbs wildly as I feel arousal seep from me in a gush that I can't even control.

I keep squeezing my eyes shut and then opening them, trying to block everything else out before giving in to the fierce desire to watch him take me apart like this. He doesn't look up at me, focused entirely on his task as he pushes me closer and closer to the inferno I know is waiting.

My whole body is tingling, a warm rush of pleasure spreading through me in what I know is a precursor to an orgasm, and I dig my heels into the floor as my mouth falls open.

And then, finally, Rome bites.

His teeth sink into my thigh just like his cock might sink into my pussy, solid and smooth and invasive but so, so welcome.

My breath stops as the pleasure inside me finally crests, and I tremble all over as Rome slides two thick fingers inside me. He can already tell I'm wet and slick for him, so he doesn't go slow, doesn't ease me into it. He just fucks me with them hard and fast as his lips clamp around my thigh and his throat moves, welcoming the blood that fills his mouth.

Ecstasy keeps crashing through me, the height of the orgasm seeming to last forever instead of cresting and fading like it normally does. Some insane part of me wonders if he's *drinking* my pleasure, consuming it right along with my blood, tasting and devouring everything he's making me feel.

When the waves of sensation finally stop slamming into me, my body goes lax against the stone. My eyelids are only half open, but I force my eyes to focus as I watch Rome slowly release my inner thigh from his mouth. Streaks of red stain his lips and teeth as he drags his tongue over my skin, cleaning up most of the blood and sealing the wounds. His fingers are still buried inside me, and for the first time, he looks up to meet my gaze as he draws them out and laps at them too.

Watching the red of my blood mix with the slick, clear fluid of my arousal sends a visceral reaction tearing through me. It's too strong for me to even identify it.

Is it desire? Revulsion? Horror? Need?

Maybe it's all of those mixed together, existing simultaneously and creating an emotion that wouldn't even exist outside of this exact situation.

"Rome," I say again. It's not a command or a plea. I don't know what it is, I just know that I still need *something*.

His tongue slides out to lick his lips, gathering the last bits of my cream and my blood. Then he moves, crawling up my body with the kind of speed only a vampire can manage. This time, he tears a hell of a lot more than my panties. His fingers grasp the bodice of my dress and rip, and the thing comes apart in his hands like it's made of goddamn tissue paper. I'm naked in seconds, and before I can register the chill of the air on my body, Rome drops his head, finding my breasts with his hungry, demanding mouth.

I clutch at his hair, biting my lip so hard I'm afraid I'll draw more blood, and he growls against my skin. I try to pull his shirt off, or his pants, but he won't let me. He refuses to draw back enough to let me get them off, and after I try for the third time, he grunts and sits back. Instead of reaching for his clothes, he grabs my hips and flips me over.

My heart lurches, my body instinctively tensing as I steady myself on my hands and knees. There's a rustling sound behind me, and I look back to realize that Rome still hasn't taken his damn clothes off—but he's shoved his pants down far enough to free his cock.

Holy fuck.

It's pierced all the way along the shaft, barbells that cut across the bottom of his length in a Jacob's Ladder. He's long and thick and hard, and the metal of his cock piercings catch the light just like the piercing in his nose does as he moves closer to me. He holds my gaze as he grabs my hips with both hands, finding my slick entrance with the head of his cock.

Then he slams inside me.

My whole body rocks forward, a guttural grunt falling from my lips as my pussy clenches around him. I can feel every one of his piercings dragging against my walls, and my head droops as he draws back and thrusts in again, using his hold on my hips to guide me back and forth on his cock.

He fucks me hard and fast, making me think that all that teasing he did to me earlier got to him too. He fucks me like he couldn't hold back or slow down even if he wanted to, like he can't help himself. Even when my pussy clamps down like a vise around him, he still doesn't stop, shortening his strokes and digging his fingers into my hips as he keeps pounding into me.

With a whispered scream, I come in a blinding rush, and he buries himself inside me one more time as his cock pulses and jerks. I expect him to pull out or maybe collapse on top of me, but he draws out partway and then slides in again as a trail of our combined arousal slides down my leg. He keeps doing that, keeps moving in and out of me as if he really and truly *can't* stop.

My head stops spinning after a while, my vision clearing and my breath returning to semi-normal as he thrusts gently.

"I wanted you," he murmurs, and I know I'm the *you* he's talking about, but I don't even know if he's speaking to me right now. It sounds more like he's talking to himself. "Even when I knew I shouldn't. I knew you were trouble." He makes a low sound that's almost a laugh. "I was wrong about what *kind* of trouble, but I knew."

I want to ask him what he knew and how he knew it, and why he thought he shouldn't want me. But before I can say anything, he slides all the way out of me. Lifting me up, he gathers me in his arms and deposits me on my back on the bed.

I gaze up at him as he straightens. His cock is still hard, jutting out over his pants, which hang low on his hips. It's slick with his own cum and my sticky wetness, and as I watch, he finally reaches up with one hand and tugs his shirt off. His muscles are thick and well-defined, his arms bulging and his abs contracting as he reaches down to shove his pants off next.

Part of me wonders why he's bothering to get naked after the sex, but another part of me already knows the answer. The part of me that can feel the thread of tension between us, still unbroken even after the intensity of our first fuck, knows the truth.

This isn't over.

We're not done.

As if summoned by my words, Rome crawls up onto the bed with me. I spread my legs for him immediately, and he braces himself over me, his hips between my thighs. He's looking at me the same way he did when he had his hand around my throat earlier. Or... *almost* the same way. His gaze is just as intense as it was then, but there's something else behind it now. As I'm trying to figure out what that is, he reaches down between us, fisting his wet cock and bringing it to my entrance. He drags the tip over my clit a few times, stoking the fire inside me and proving that it hasn't burned away everything yet.

There's still plenty of tinder to fuel this flame.

Keeping his gaze locked on mine, he presses into me.

Where the first time was fast and hard, this time is slow and so deliberate it feels like he's claiming every inch of me as I stretch around him.

When he's fully rooted inside me, he takes my hands, lacing our fingers together before pressing the backs of my hands to the mattress above my head. I can't touch him like this, can't stroke the broad muscles of his chest or shoulders or back, can't grab his ass to pull him closer or run my fingers through the rich brown of his hair.

But I think there's a reason for that. I don't think he *wants* me to touch him like that, even though he obviously craves the closeness of our bodies. We're rocking in unison, our sweaty skin pressed together, our lips so close that our inhales and exhales combine. His fingers are tight around mine as if he's trying to weld our hands together, but that's the only touch he allows me.

I take it, squeezing his hands back and locking my legs around his hips, undulating beneath him to match his rhythm.

I'm going to come again. I can feel it building in the base of my spine, as inevitable as death and fucking taxes. But I don't let it come too fast, clenching my toes and taking deep, gasping breaths every time I'm almost at the peak. I wait until my body is shaking, so full of pleasure it feels like it might burst. I wait until every brush of his skin against mine feels like lightning.

I wait until Rome is right there with me.

Only when he lets out a deep groan, his cock swelling inside me as the first lashes of his hot cum fill me up, do I let myself go. I come with him, straining against his hold on my hands as I lift my head from the mattress and crush my lips to his, locking my ankles together and grinding against him as he spills inside me.

And as he slumps against me, his body warm and hard and heavy against mine, the thread of tension between us finally snaps.

CHAPTER TWENTY-ONE

We lie like that for several long moments. My entire body is limp, except for my hands, which are still clutching Rome's so hard I'm afraid it might take a crowbar to separate us.

Finally, he drags in a breath through his nose and lifts his head up. We both unpeel our fingers from the knotted tangle of digits, and then Rome rolls off me, settling onto the mattress at my side. He pulls me against him, and I lie cradled in his embrace, my head resting on his chest.

If he were human, I'd be listening to his heartbeat.

It should bother me that there's nothing to hear, but for some reason, it doesn't. Whatever else he is, he's Rome—the honorable vampire. The vampire who somehow pissed off an entire nest and earned his way back into the fold. I don't want to know how he did the latter, but somehow I don't think any human paid unnecessarily for it.

He strokes my hair, and I close my eyes, relishing in the brief moment of calm and connection.

"Why did you come here?" he asks me after a while. His voice is quiet, almost soft.

I could lie to him, but I don't want to. He already knows so much. If I don't tell him, he's going to come to his own conclusions. The idea that he'll be murderously angry at whatever those conclusions may be doesn't bother me as much as the thought of him assuming that I used him. Which, to a certain extent, I did—but I think he'll understand why once he knows the truth. At least, I hope he will.

"Nathan is my brother," I murmur. "The tall, skinny tribute with the prison tattoos."

"Ah." He sighs. "The one you asked me to protect. Is the other your sister? Cousin?"

I shake my head. "No. Just a woman who's doing what she thinks is best to make sure that her mother never has to suffer."

He tightens his arm around me, comforting me. I return the embrace, then pull away. If I'm going to get through this, I'm going to need to not be distracted by his touch. I tuck my knees up to my chest and hug them.

"Nathan got himself in a lot of trouble, but not enough to end up here on his own. He was played, funneled into position and coerced into accepting. He doesn't deserve to be here, and he won't last long if he stays. He's not —strong."

It hurts me to say it out loud. I don't like thinking of my brother as weak, even if it is the truth.

Rome stands and reaches a hand down to pull me to my feet. We're both still naked, and cum is dripping down my leg, but there's no self-consciousness at all. After what just happened between us, I'm way past the point of feeling vulnerable with him just because I'm not wearing any clothes. Somehow, I feel like he's seen more of me than almost anyone else I've ever known, and I don't mean the outside of me.

I mean the *inside*.

The shit that truly matters.

"You're here to rescue him," Rome murmurs, stepping closer to me. "From us, or from himself?"

I laugh a little, soft and sad. "Both, I guess. But I can't save him from himself while he's in danger here. I need to help him. He needs—he deserves a chance to have a real life."

He strokes my face, his thumb trailing down my cheek and over my jaw. He tips my head up, and his eyes glow as he gazes down at me. The usual hardness in him is melted away in this moment, leaving him soft and warm and sad. He presses his forehead to mine, cradling my head in his hand. He kisses me gently, first one cheek, then the other, then takes my mouth with his.

He kisses me like he's pouring everything he is into the gesture, like it hurts him but he can't stop.

I've never been kissed like this before, but I'm not an idiot. I know what it means.

He's telling me goodbye.

My heart hurts. I cling to him, memorizing the feel of his body, the taste of his mouth. I'm vulnerable, but so is he. It strikes me, ironically, that I've never felt safer.

He pulls away before I'm ready for him to, and I can feel his walls go up. It makes the room feel cold, and the few inches of space between us feel like a gaping chasm. I wrap my arms around myself and shiver.

"I will not tell anyone that you are a slayer," he says in a formal tone that sounds like an oath. "But if leaving is your mission, you should complete it soon. If I was able to figure out what you are, others will too—and they won't have reason to show restraint."

I wonder what he would say if I ask him what his reasons are, but I feel like our private altercations and conversations have already gone on too long. Someone is bound to notice. It's not usual for vampires to visit tributes in their rooms. Too intimate, I suppose.

Rome hesitates for a moment, looking like he wants to say more. There's a flicker of something in his eyes—some memory or emotion—but it's gone as quickly as it came, leaving me with no idea what it was or where it came from.

He dresses quickly, then turns back to me and nods his head slightly, stiff and formal.

A moment later, I'm alone in my room again.

I know he's right. I'm out of time, and it's now or never. It's well into the afternoon by now—the equivalent of the middle of night around here.

After cleaning up quickly, I go to the wardrobe to grab clothes, mentally cursing the fact that I have no tactical wear here. It's just a bunch of fucking dresses, but I tug on the one that I think will be easiest to move in.

It'll have to do.

Turning away from the heavy wardrobe, I start to gather my things to go get Nathan, then stop.

Jessica.

Even if she isn't in immediate danger from James, she certainly isn't out of the woods. Like Nathan, she isn't strong enough to last long around here. Maybe she has the guts, but physically, she gives all the vibes of a small, adorable, defenseless prey animal. If *I* can sense that, being nothing but a human hunter, how much stronger is that sense to the vampires? The worst of them will bleed her dry. Even the best of them will be hard-pressed to keep her safely alive for the length of her contract.

I know she's going to argue with me, but I have to try. Moving carefully and quietly, I sneak out of my room and down the hall, past the bathroom and Winona's room, as well as the rooms of several other tributes. I tap lightly on Jessica's door and don't wait for a response before I open it. She's sitting on her bed, and she raises her eyebrows and smiles softly when she sees me.

"Hey. Can't sleep?" she asks, understanding filling her hazel eyes. "I totally get it. This backwards schedule's been a pain to get used to. I thought it would be like jet lag, easy to get over after a few days, but my internal clock is all messed up."

Not even bothering to answer her question, I close the door silently behind me and then cross the room in a few strides. I sit down beside her and take her hand, squeezing it harder than I mean to.

She gives me a surprised look. "What's wrong?"

"I'm getting out of here," I murmur, my voice shaking. "I'm rescuing my brother. That's the whole reason I came here in the first place."

Her eyes widen. "You're what?"

"How would you like to see your mom again?" I ask her, talking fast because I can already see the resistance on her face. "Hug her and talk to her and hold her hand? I can get you out of here too, Jessica. Come with me."

She stares at me for a long moment as she processes what I just said. Then she throws her arms around me and hugs me.

"Oh my god, Darcy. I had no idea." Her voice is a hushed whisper. "I... thank you."

I hug her back fiercely, squeezing my eyes shut against a wave of too many emotions.

"I have to get some things from my room," I tell her, choosing not to mention that the *things* I need are weapons capable of decapitating any vampire in the place. "Grab what you need and come with me."

Jessica sighs and lets her arms drop, leaning back to smile at me sadly. She shakes her head.

"Thank you for trying to get me out of here," she says quietly. "But I can't." She blinks rapidly, her eyes glistening. "I hope you're able to get your brother out of here in one piece. I really do. I'm going to miss you so much. But I can't go with you."

I frown at her, my heart sinking. "Jessica—"

She shakes her head, her lips trembling. "If I violate the terms of the contract, they'll kill my mother. Or remove their support and let her die slowly, which would be infinitely worse. The doctor they hired put my mom on this experimental drug—it's stupid expensive and ridiculously difficult to get—but it's working. She can walk with a cane again. She can grab things too, if they're big enough for her to get a good grip on. She still can't write or open pill bottles, and her vision is still spotty, but she's getting better."

I clench my jaw, hating that this sweet, selfless girl is caught between saving her mother's life and her own. It should never have fucking come to this.

"We'll figure it out," I promise. "Whatever they're paying for her care, I'll come up with a way to get it. I'll protect her from retaliation, and you too. It's not going to be easy, but we can make it happen. Don't you want her to be able to see you when she gets her sight back?"

Maybe that was manipulative, but the determination in Jessica's eyes is making me panic.

She shakes her head sadly. "You can't save everybody, Darcy. No matter how much you want to. Let's face it, the vampires are the only ones with enough money and power to do what they're doing for her. I can't mess that up. I won't. She doesn't deserve to live in pain."

"Neither do *you*," I say desperately, but I can see that the argument is over. Jessica smiles at me and squeezes my hands again.

"You can't keep everyone safe," she repeats. "Sometimes you have to choose. I can't leave—so go save your brother. He needs you."

My stomach clenches. Her mind is made up; I can see it in every line of her face. She's one of the softest, sweetest people I've ever met, but she's clearly just as damn stubborn as I am.

More and more arguments tumble through my head, but I know none of them will convince her. None of them are strong enough to bend reality to my will.

I get up stiffly, forcing my unwilling feet to move. I don't want to leave her. I always thought of Jessica as my best friend in this place, but now that it comes down to it, I realize with a shock that she's become my best friend, *period*.

Jessica gets to her feet too, calm everywhere except her eyes. She's as worried about me as I am about her, but she isn't fighting me to make me stay. Maybe she has more faith in me than I do in either of us. Maybe that's her strength—or her weakness. I can't tell the difference anymore.

She hugs me so hard my bones creak, and I return the gesture. I have the sudden, stupid impulse to pick her up and carry her out of here, as if that wouldn't attract way too much attention. She's shaking. I wonder if she has the impulse to knock me out and keep me there. I guess we all have different ways of staying safe.

"Don't die," she orders, her voice hoarse. "Don't you dare die."

"I won't if you won't," I say, then stop talking before my voice breaks.

Her face is wet with tears when I pull away. Maybe mine is too, I don't know. I give her hands a final squeeze. She nods solemnly. I want to say something more, but what is there left to say?

We are, each of us, marching knowingly into mortal danger and probable death.

With pain burning a hole in my heart, I slip back down the hall and strap my weapons on.

CHAPTER TWENTY-TWO

My random wanderings have given me a better understanding of the palace layout. Vampires aren't straightforward creatures, and the Baltimore underground is a twisted ruin. I've learned that getting to the men's quarters undetected is infinitely easier if I walk away from it first, toward the dining hall, then keep going until I come to the passage which cuts diagonally across the back corner. From there, it's a bit of a maze, but I've wandered it enough times to know where I'm going.

As I walk on silent feet, I pass the little alcove where Connor kissed me, and a wave of sadness threatens to break my focus. I don't want to think about the fact that I'll never see him again.

I want to go find him. I want to get him out of here, have him come live with me somewhere sunny and bright like his personality.

But that would kill him. And he, eventually, would kill me.

I keep forgetting he's a vampire. He seems so fucking human to me, and it's not fair that he's trapped as an undead monster. If there's a way to un-turn a vampire, I've never heard of it. The magic that makes them what they are also keeps them alive. I can't imagine a vampire,—especially one who had been mortally wounded in the moments before his turning—would survive a reversal, even if one was possible.

It's pointless to keep thinking about him, but I can't seem to get him out of my mind.

It's the vampire magic, I tell myself. Not that I believe it.

Still, the thought gives me hope. If it's just magic, it will fade. Then I'll be able to shove all of these feelings and memories into a box in my mind and lock it up tight like I've done with so many other things.

I make it to Nathan's room without seeing or hearing anyone. More importantly, I make it there without being seen. I don't bother knocking this time. I just slip right in. My brother jerks up in bed and then scrambles to his feet as I close the door, looking foggy-eyed and tousled. Unlike Jessica, he was definitely asleep.

"What's going on?" he asks, his words slurred and his voice rough.

"Shoes. Shirt. We're leaving."

"Wh—bu—Mimi," he protests. "I'm not ready. I'm still sick from those damn women."

"You've jumped fences with the cops on your ass after being up for four days spun out of your mind on meth and dehydrated within an inch of your life," I snap briskly. "Get your damn shoes on."

He frowns at me but he does what I tell him. He shrugs into a button-down shirt—all the buttons have been ripped off, and god, I really want to know how or when that happened—and flattens his hair as best he can. Then he shrugs at me defiantly.

"There."

I roll my eyes. He's going to attract all kinds of negative attention looking like that, or at least, he will if anyone sees us. But if it gets to that point, it won't matter what he's wearing. Besides, I don't have time to get him dressed properly. I grab his wrist and open the door slightly, just enough to see that the hall is empty.

"Why are we doing this now?" he whispers.

I glare at him and put a finger to my lips. He shuts up, but he doesn't look happy about it. I'm glad we have to be quiet right now. I'm not real thrilled at the prospect of admitting to him that it's my fault we have to leave now. I'm the one who blew our cover, and that doesn't sit right with the part of me that's always insisted I've got this under control.

Even though Rome said he wouldn't tell anybody, I

can't really rely on him to keep that promise. He could always change his mind. As far as vampire societal law goes, he'd be well within his rights to do that. Like he said, he has a *duty*.

I drag Nathan down the hall, leading him swiftly down corridors I've spent weeks memorizing. It takes longer than I'd like, but we don't hit any dead ends or get lost in any passages, and after several agonizing minutes, we step into a little hallway that connects to the crossed hallways in the center of the palace.

I never managed to figure out the full code, but I'll have to make this work with the intel I have. Out of six numbers, I have four, but I have some solid guesses of what the missing two numbers might be, based on where I saw various vampire's fingers hovering over the keypad.

Dammit, I should have asked Rome, but he probably wouldn't have told me. His loyalty might be flexible enough to turn a blind eye to my escape attempt, but I doubt he would betray the other vampires outright.

God, Rome.

The thought of the gruff, enigmatic vampire seems to open up a wound in my chest.

I can't believe I'll never see him again. Maybe he'll get himself banished again, and I'll meet him on the streets. The image of me recognizing him just as I drive a stake into his chest sends a shiver of horror through my stomach, followed by a wave of sadness. He's the enemy. He always will be, for the rest of my life and long after I'm dead.

"You good?" Nathan asks, his eyes glinting in the dim light as he studies my face.

I scowl, hiding whatever expression it is that he's reacting to.

"I'm fine," I tell him. "Keep moving. We're almost there."

CHAPTER TWENTY-THREE

It only takes us another minute to reach the sleek elevator. Our ticket out of this place, if we can figure out how to open it.

"Watch my back," I whisper to Nathan.

"Where does this go?" he asks.

"Up into an office building. It's the middle of the day topside. They probably won't have vampire guards at every door and intersection up there, not in broad daylight. Now shut up, I'm trying to remember the code."

"Remember" is a bit of a stretch. The numbers I know are etched so deeply into my brain that I'll never forget them. But for the two missing digits, there's nothing to recall since I don't actually know them.

The keypad code is six digits. Zero-nine-three-something-something-four.

I'm pretty sure the fourth digit is either a one or a two, and I think the fifth might be a seven or an eight.

Fuck it. I'll just have to guess until I get it right, and pray it doesn't set off an alarm.

I punch some numbers in, trying the first possible combination.

Nothing.

The door doesn't open, but no alarm goes off either, so I take that as the small victory it is and keep trying.

It turns out, I was wrong. The fifth digit is a *five*, but after several minutes of cursing under my breath and punching the keypad with shaking fingers, I finally enter the right combo. The arrow on the keypad turns green, pointing upward like a beacon leading to freedom, and I let out a ragged breath.

The elevator door slides open, and I grab Nathan by the arm and haul him in after me.

I want to feel relieved, but despite the brief moment of victory, I know we're not out of the woods yet. I punch the button for the street level floor—there are two floors between here and there—then stand with my back pressed against the cold glass. Nathan's giving me a worried look, chewing on his lower lip.

"What?"

"How did you know about this?" he whispers. "How do you know where it goes?"

"Prince Bloodsucker took me up here once."

Ouch. I didn't think calling him that would hurt. It's not like I'm in love with him or anything... but I had a connection with him.

Maybe I just need to connect with more *human* people. I don't really make a habit of it. I never considered it a weakness before now, but maybe I should have. Loneliness leaves you vulnerable to rotten connections.

And seeing Bastian as anything but a monster is a mistake. Just because he's been hurt before, just because he's experienced the exact same pain I have, that doesn't mean he's a good person.

It doesn't mean I should allow myself to miss him if—when—I get Nathan out of this place.

As I try to drag myself from the memory of what it felt like to have Bastian's solid arms around me, his hand resting on my stomach and his face buried in the crook of my neck, the elevator chimes suddenly.

I stiffen.

This isn't right. We shouldn't be stopping. We aren't at the ground floor yet. Keeping my gaze locked on the doors, I step forward so that Nathan is behind me, reaching back to hand him one of my blades. I raise my other knife as the twin doors slide open.

"What—" Nathan starts to say, then stops.

The five vampires outside the elevator door stare at us. We stare back.

For a second, nobody does anything.

Then we explode into motion.

Striking like a cobra, I leap forward and jab at the "close door" button at the exact moment that one of the vampires hisses and launches himself into the elevator. The rest of them follow, practically landing on top of each other, fangs bared, mouths spewing inhuman snarls.

One grabs my shoulders and lunges at my throat, but he ends up swallowing my knife instead. It bursts through the back of his head, coated in slick, dark blood. More blood and foam gurgle past his reaching fangs, smothering his furious growls. I don't have enough room to yank the blade out and stick it where it'll do some real damage, so I kick him as hard as I can. He slams into the button panel hard enough to shove my knife forward, but not quite out of his mouth.

It's fucking disgusting, but I don't have time to dwell on that because there's another vampire attacking me from the other side. He goes for my throat, and I duck down, letting his face smash into the glass wall behind me. If I never hear vampire fangs screeching down glass again, it'll be too soon.

From this vantage, all I can see of Nathan is his feet, but the frustrated grunts of our attackers and the darkly metallic scent of vampire blood in the air tell me that he's holding his own... so far, anyway.

The elevator chimes again.

I throw a kick at the vampire nearest to me, connecting

with his chest and sending him flying out through the elevator doors as they open. The rest of us tumble out after him. Deepthroat vamp jerks my knife out of his mouth and throws it aside. A mistake on his part. I grab it as it skitters across the floor, then leap up, take aim, and stab.

I should have wiped it off first. The slick film of blood and foam compromises my grip, and I miss his heart. There's a scuffling sound behind me, and I try to keep myself alert for a sneak attack as I recalibrate my target and go for the vamp's head. He hisses and leaps out of the way, too fast even with a chest wound.

"Stop, tribute!" a voice from behind me shrieks.

"No! Don't stop, Mimi! Run!" The sound of Nathan's panicked tone has me spinning around, and my heart lodges in my throat when I see him.

They have him. He's caught.

A vampire holds him in a one-armed chokehold. His other hand curls around Nathan's throat, his claw-like fingernails denting Nathan's skin. As I watch, beads of blood pop up under the claws just as beads of sweat pop out on Nathan's brow.

"Give up, sweetie," the vampire drawls, grinning darkly at me over Nathan's shoulder. "Or the boy dies."

"Don't do it," Nathan gasps, wincing at the pain in his neck. "Run, Mikka. Get out of here. I'll be fine."

"You're a liar," I say around the lump in my throat. "And an idiot if you think I'm leaving you."

There's nothing else I can do. I'm pretty good at attacking without telegraphing my movements, but there's no way I could end this fight before Nathan dies. This is why I try so hard to maintain the element of surprise when I go up against vamps on the outside, and why I always used to hunt alone.

I slowly put my blades on the floor and raise my hands as the vampire holding him chuckles. As soon as I straighten, another bloodsucker grabs me from behind, locking me in a chokehold. I could probably get out of it if I tried, but I won't. Nathan would be dead before I could manage it.

"Let me kill her, Ahmir," the one holding me growls, tightening his grip around my neck. "I won't be talkin' right for a week after that stunt."

Ah. That's why my back is wet. His slowly closing neck wound is bleeding all over me. Gross.

"Nah," the one holding Nathan says. *Ahmir*. His grin widens, and it makes him look even more evil somehow. "The Council of Elders will decide what to do with them. Roy, grab those weapons. The prince will want to know what his precious tributes have been up to."

Fuck.

Cold sweat drips down my spine, and I drag my feet in spite of myself. The stark terror gripping my heart has very little to do with the room full of vicious, ancient vampires I'm about to face. It has to do with the fact that one of those vicious, ancient vampires is Bastian—whose parents were killed by hunters.

He was vulnerable with me when he told me that. He shared a part of himself I doubt he lets many people see.

And now he's going to hate me even more when he finds out what I am.

CHAPTER TWENTY-FOUR

The vampire guards who caught us call for backup quickly and send several of the new arrivals to alert the Elders and the prince about what's going on.

By the time we reach the council chambers, most of the vampires I usually see behind the high table in the dining hall are already there, and I curse inwardly. If I had any hopes of getting a small amount of respite or another chance to escape before we were hauled before the vampire court to face justice, they're quickly dashed.

The vampire behind me shoves me to my knees, and Nathan drops down beside me. From where I kneel, I can't see Bastian's eyes. Maybe that's for the best, since I don't think I'd be able to look him in the face anyway.

Damn him. Damn this whole mess.

The rug looks thick and lush under the long table, but the floor beneath me is hard, unforgiving marble. The room is full of vampires, and more are filing in. Whatever word got sent out after Nathan and I were captured, it must've reached pretty much the whole damn hive.

"What is the meaning of this?" Bastian demands. "What's going on?" He isn't loud, but his voice rolls across the room, full of power.

"We caught these two trying to escape," Nathan's captor says. "Blood tributes, both of 'em. The female's a hunter."

There's a long pause, then Bastian speaks. I can hear the restraint in his voice, like a tight rubber band. "These are serious charges, Ahmir. Bring them to their feet. Let me see the accused."

They aren't gentle about it. I try to keep my head down, but the vampire holding me is having none of it. He jerks my head back using a fistful of my hair, forcing me to make eye contact with the prince. Bastian's face is a mask, but his eyes—maybe I'm imagining the pain I see in their depths. Maybe it's just anger.

Or maybe, like me, he can no longer tell the difference between the two.

"What proof do you have that she's a hunter?" he asks, his voice dangerously quiet.

Ahmir jerks his head at the vampire who collected my weapons from the floor. The guy dumps my curved blades on the table hard enough to make me wince. That really isn't good for them—not that it matters now, I guess.

"She might have more on her," the guy holding me says helpfully. He slides his free hand over my body, groping me with bruising fingers. "I can search her, if you like. Everywhere."

Bastian narrows his eyes, his nostrils flaring a little as his jaw tightens. "No. Just do your job and restrain her. Raven, remove any remaining weapons."

A female vampire glides over to me. She moves her hands over me with a wholly clinical briskness, reaching into places better left alone without a hint of shame. When she's finished, she glances back up at Bastian. "She's clean. The two knives must've been all she carried."

"We cannot allow this rebellion to stand," the Elder to Bastian's right says. "They must be punished. Thoroughly. We must make an example of them, lest others follow in their ill-fated footsteps."

His voice is a low grumble. He's old—like, *obviously* old. He must have been over seventy when he was turned.

The woman to Bastian's left nods her head energetically. She looks like a teenager everywhere except her eyes, which are deep, ancient, and terrifying.

"Death," the old man says heavily. "Public. Waste of good meat, but..." He shrugs. He doesn't look as bothered as his words suggest.

The not-a-teenager on Bastian's other side scoffs. "Death. How boring. No, no, I have a much better idea."

Her eyes glow, and she gazes for a long while at

Nathan's face. He pales, beads of sweat popping out across his face. She's drunk from him before, I realize belatedly—she has a personal investment in him. The hair on the back of my neck stands up, and I look behind me quickly. The room has filled up with vampires and there, standing in the crowd just behind Nathan, are Althea and Maureen. Their teeth are bared, their eyes hungry. Althea leans forward, closing the space between her and Nathan, and inhales deeply through her nose.

The woman beside Bastian smiles a predator's smile as her eyes twinkle maliciously.

"I do not believe that your timing is coincidental, tribute," she says to Nathan, addressing him without really speaking to him. "You run from those who would bond you to them as their own, clearly hoping to escape before the ceremony. Silly human." Now she looks at him, her eyes black and lifeless as a shark. "We need no *ceremony* to bind you. Vampires are theatrical by nature—but pragmatic by necessity."

She doesn't wait for Bastian to weigh in, just snaps her fingers three times. A lower level vampire disappears from the room and appears again moments later, holding a crystal tray topped with a crystal chalice. Both items are encrusted with blood red teardrop-shaped rubies.

I can see the liquid in the glass, but I can't tell what it is. The color and texture seem to change as I stare at it. One instant, it's blue smoke, the next it's flaming orange ice. The only consistent thing about it is the power it radiates, a magic wave which undulates over the crowd.

The vampires nearest to it seem to come more wide awake, their postures shifting as their eyes dilate, and I have the very definite sense that many of them are aroused.

"Althea. Maureen. Step forward," the female vampire says briskly.

"Yes, Lizbeth," they murmur in unison, making goosebumps prickle over my skin. Jesus, I hate it when vampires do that.

They do as they're told, shaking and practically salivating, their attention caught between Nathan and the chalice. Nathan looks terrified, glancing with wide eyes from one woman to the other. Finally deciding that Althea is the bigger threat, he edges away from her, which takes him nearer to Maureen. Realizing his mistake, he freezes.

It was only a tiny thing, just a split-second, but that was enough. The vampire running the show, Lizbeth, seems to have seen the same thing I did. It pleases her, and she claps her hands.

"Oh what fun! It has been so long. *Too* long"—that part is directed at Bastian with a subtly petulant expression—"since we've seen a tribute bonded to one who terrifies him so. It adds spice to the atmosphere, don't you think? Puts everything in the right order. Seasons the blood, you know."

Guilt and terror for Nathan crush into my gut. I fight

the urge to be sick all over the floor, then wonder if maybe that would make them less likely to bond me to someone. By her logic, the perfect vampire for me would be James. That thought sends an extra wave of terror through me, but it pales in comparison to what I'm feeling for Nathan.

I try to catch Bastian's eye, but he won't look at me. His attention is on Nathan, his expression even more blank and impassive than it usually is during all the dinners he's presided over since I came here. He might as well be carved from fucking ice right now.

"Althea," Lizbeth says. "The tribute is yours."

I assume the blonde one is Maureen, since she's the one who snarls in response to Lizbeth's words. The curvy brunette is preening like a peacock, blithely ignoring Maureen's wordless threats.

"Enough, Maureen," Lizbeth snaps. "Take your leave."

"He's mine!" Maureen hisses through her teeth.

"If you'd taken care of him," the old man says blandly, "perhaps he would not have run. It would do you well to remember not to break your toys in the future."

Maureen hisses again, wordlessly like a cat, then stalks out of the room. I'm shaking. Nathan isn't—he isn't moving at all anymore. He's standing perfectly still, rigid, his eyes laser-focused on the crystal tray. Lizbeth rises from her seat and stands in front of the long table, and the servant follows her.

"Althea." She glances at the brunette and makes a sharp summoning gesture.

The brunette vampire moves to her side, and for the first time, I see Althea as she really is. Not a petty, soft sex kitten, but a vicious, brutal predator. It's in the way she moves, the anticipation in her eyes, the way she dismisses the whole room to focus solely on her prey. Nathan.

"Bring the tribute forward," Lizbeth orders.

"No!" I shout. I don't expect the vampires to care, but I need Nathan to. I need him to move. To *fight*.

My voice breaks whatever spell he's been under, and he starts to resist, struggling against the vampires, flinging his head back and trying to break his captor's nose. I fight too, more to pull manpower—vampire power—from his struggle than out of any real effort to escape. I know they won't let me go, but if Nathan's too much trouble, maybe they'll focus on me.

I'm pinned in moments. Someone punches my head hard enough to screw up my equilibrium, and for a few seconds, there seem to be twice as many vampires in the room.

"Make her watch," Lizbeth's voice cuts through the fog in my head, her icy tone freezing me from the inside out.

Two vamps drag me back to my feet, and I see with a pang of disappointment that it was all for nothing. They have Nathan on his knees in front of the big table, his arms held uselessly behind him, his head tilted back. Althea stands before him, her expression solemn and pleased, though her eyes blaze with hunger. Lizbeth stands behind and between them, holding the chalice.

Nathan is struggling for his life, making his captors curse and growl with the effort to keep him still. Lizbeth raises the chalice, then frowns and lowers it again. She casts an apologetic smile around, then focuses her attention on me.

"There's a verse that usually accompanies this," she says as if she's gossiping to a girlfriend. "But it isn't necessary. Hold him still."

That last part is an order to the vampire guards, who have been trying to do just that. Two more join their efforts, and between the four of them, they get Nathan into place. He clenches his jaw, sealing his lips closed, glaring defiantly up at Lizbeth. I've never been prouder of him.

But his defiance isn't enough to stop what's coming. In a move almost too quick for me to see, she seizes his face in her hands and forces his mouth open.

"Tribute—by the magic of the Cruor Chalice and the traditions of the Vampire Court, I hereby bind you to Althea Antoinette Andreanakis, your mistress and one love from this moment until your last mortal breath."

As she speaks, Lizbeth pours the liquid into his mouth. He's fighting, not swallowing, but nothing splashes out of his mouth. She empties the chalice into him, every last drop. I can see it moving down his throat even though he's doing nothing to help it along.

When the chalice is empty, Lizbeth steps back. Althea takes her place and kneels in front of Nathan, a posture that would almost seem lovingly submissive if it weren't for the killer gleam in her eye. She bares her teeth, tilting her head dramatically back, then sinks her fangs into him.

She isn't gentle. Not even close. She *gnaws* on him, letting blood spill messily down his neck to his shoulder, making disgusting animal grunts the whole time.

I can't breathe. My chest has locked up so tight that my lungs will no longer accept air. I don't even know if my heart is beating.

Nathan isn't fighting anymore. There's a blissful haze over his features, and all the fight is gone from his eyes.

She has him.

She's won.

Now there's no one to stop her from killing him or torturing him as she pleases. I expect her to do it here and now, right in front of me, but she doesn't. Instead, she closes him up—though not with the same care or compassion that I've felt and seen from others, just a swipe of her tongue—then leans away from him.

"Who do you serve, Nathan?"

"Althea," he breathes.

My blood runs like ice. I've heard him sound like that

before, when he's in the middle of a bad spell and he finally gets his hands on a fix.

"Who do you love?" Althea asks, narrowing her eyes at me before shooting a hostile glance at the doorway. Maureen must still be watching.

"Only Althea," Nathan murmurs. "Althea, my mistress."

She grins. "Good boy," she purrs, patting him on the head. "Come along now, there's nothing interesting left to do—in here."

With blood still coating her lips and chin, she gives him a hooded look that sends shivers down my spine. I squeeze my eyes shut against the unwelcome imagery of what she could do to him in private, but open them again as she starts to drag him from the room. He's not even looking at me, too focused on his new *mistress*, but I force myself to watch him go. To witness the full brunt of my failure.

Once Nathan and Althea are gone, the atmosphere of the entire room seems to shift as, one by one, all eyes turn to me. Now *I'm* the center of attention, and it makes my blood feel like ice water.

"A hunter," the old man growls between his teeth, leaning toward me. "The same punishment cannot be meted out to her. Hunters cannot be permitted to live."

Lizbeth nods grimly. "On this we agree, Tyresius."

The rest of the Elders at the table, the ones who

haven't yet spoken, voice their own agreements. It's unanimous—except for Bastian, who still hasn't said a word.

I search for his eyes, and he finally allows me to see them, meeting my gaze. His face is hard. Impassive. That's all it takes for me to realize he won't go against the Elders in this. Even if he could, he wouldn't. I can see the pain in his eyes, the resolve in his spine when his gaze brushes over my weapons.

His parents were slaughtered in front of him by the likes of me. I wonder if the weapons they used were the same.

I breathe, calling on my hunter zen. I'm not planning to hunt, but I've seen enough death to know that I don't want to die panicking. I straighten, battered and bruised, and meet Bastian's gaze defiantly. The least I can do is make sure this memory sticks with him for the next couple hundred years.

"Did you not hear, tribute?" Tyresius demands. "You are to be put to death for your crimes."

"To me and mine, I have committed no crimes," I shoot back, letting the truth of it ring through my voice. "I took my life in my hands the moment I chose to defend humanity from the likes of you."

He snarls at me and makes a sharp gesture in the air. Vampires move in from all sides, jockeying for position around me. My stomach drops as I realize they're going to tear me apart. I've seen the aftermath of that, once. There wasn't much left but a zipper, some hair, and a couple fingernails. Everything else had either been eaten or torn small and spread thin. The gore covered an alley from one end of the block to the other, up both sides to the rooftops. A rat ran over my foot with an eyeball in its mouth.

Bile rises in my throat at the memory, but I swallow it down and keep my eyes steady on Bastian's.

The feral, animalistic growls all around me grow louder as the vamps creep closer. They're breathing on me, licking my skin at my pulse, teasing me. They want me broken with terror before they get rid of me. They won't get the satisfaction. I swear to god, they won't.

"What? No begging? No remorse?" Lizbeth sounds offended.

At some unseen signal, the vampires fall back half a step. I turn my gaze from Bastian to the too-young looking vampire and smile at her. She doesn't like that, which makes me smile wider.

"Beg? For what? A chance to be somebody's helpless pet?" I spit the last word, and she wrinkles her nose. I won't even bother addressing her "remorse" comment. I have nothing to feel guilty about except my failure to protect Nathan.

Lizbeth's gaze darts from my face to the faces of the tributes standing unobtrusively against one wall, and then to the vampires gathered around me. I can feel their fierce attention, their hunger, held back only by the command of the vampire court stationed at the table.

She scowls and raises her hand. She's going to signal them to attack. Bastian won't stop them, I know he won't. I don't see Rome or Connor in the crowd, and I can't decide if I'm glad or sad about that. I think it might break my heart to see them turn their backs on me too.

"Stop," Tyresius says suddenly.

I blink at the ancient looking vampire, shocked out of my fear for a moment. Lizbeth turns to face him, looking as surprised as I feel.

"I beg your pardon?" she hisses.

"I don't like beggars." Tyresius scowls at me. "But I prefer them to martyrs."

He nods toward the tributes in the audience, then shakes his head. I follow his gaze, my heart constricting. Fuck, I didn't realize any humans had entered the room. It's definitely not *all* of the tributes, just some, and they're cowering in a tight group watching everything play out before them. I don't see Jessica, thank fuck, but I do see Winona. She's white as a damn sheet.

"So? What do you suggest?" one of the other Elders asks.

Tyresius is quiet for a long moment, then he smiles. It's not a pleasant smile.

"The hunter will become the hunted," he says softly, like he's quoting from somewhere. "There is only one fate worse than death for a vampire hunter, and that is to become the thing they hunt. If we turn her, she will be forced to become the thing she despises. What she *won't* do is become a figurehead for the slaves, a martyr for them to rally around."

"We don't call them slaves anymore," the man beside Tyresius murmurs to him.

"Perhaps that's the problem," Tyresius grumbles. "No sense of propriety anymore. I won't argue any longer. Turn her."

"No!" A harsh, panicked voice rises up from the back of the room, and I whip my head around in time to see Connor run into the council chambers.

My heart feels like it might collapse in on itself as joy and anguish mix within me at the sight of him. Connor. Sweet, sweet, too-human Connor.

"That's not fair." He shakes his head, his face stricken. "You can't do that to her!"

"Silence!" Tyresius barks.

It's not a request, it's an order—one that's carried out by the guards who pull Connor back through the crowd and out of my sight, muffling his cries for justice as they drag him from the room. The fact that he still believes in justice in these vampire-infested halls hurts my heart, and I swallow hard.

He stood up for me, even though he must know by now that I'm a vampire hunter. Even though I betrayed him too, he tried to help me. But he failed, and as I'm dragged toward the Elders' table, I pray to god they won't kill him for trying.

I don't think Rome is even here. Maybe he snuck off somewhere deep into the palace to be alone after he left my room. He probably won't even hear about this until it's already too late.

Until it's done.

True panic builds inside me like a fucking tidal wave as I fight against the vampires holding me. I was ready for the death. I made my peace with my mortality a very long time ago. But I *won't* be made a vampire. I won't. To live on the blood of humans, to become everything I despise in the world...

No. I won't let them.

"Get your hands off me!" I growl, kicking out with my shackled feet and flailing with my head. I knock a few of my captors off-balance, but they compensate too quickly. More vampire guards join the ones holding my arms. It takes five of them to carry me to the table. I would be smug about that if there was room for anything in my head except panic and despair.

They slam me onto the table and jerk my head to one side. Out of the corner of my eye, I can see Bastian.

He's looking away, gazing out over the crowd that has gathered, his eyes fixed on a spot on the far wall. Tyresius the ancient grins down at me, his eyes taking on a predatory glow. He slaps one cold, bony hand over my temple and presses the other into my collar bone hard enough to break it. I hear it pop and feel it give, but panic overrides the burst of pain.

His teeth sink into me. I barely feel them, sharp as they are. I barely feel anything.

Apparently dissatisfied with that, Tyresius shakes his head like a dog, ripping the veins and muscles in my neck until I cry out in pain and terror. He caught my jugular. I can feel the blood spurt out with every rapid beat of my heart, faster than he can swallow it. It spreads, warm and distant, under my head.

My face is cold.

My eyes won't focus.

I'm pretty sure I lost my feet somewhere, and I can't remember the last time I had them with me.

My brain is trying to find me. The room spins, first this way, then that. I want to grab hold of something, but my fingers have gone missing too.

There's a heavy black smell between my nose and my head, and it's spreading, spreading, taking me with it into the dark. I don't feel anything anymore, not even panic, not even my own heartbeat.

The last murmurs of sound fade from my ears, and I drift. I should be afraid, but I don't remember how to be.

And then...

There's an unexpected *something* in the dark, a bitter

flavor, stale and cold—the way a thirty-year-old refrigerator smells in the middle of summer, but in a thick syrup that slides over my tongue. I can feel my tongue. I swallow to get the taste out, and sensation returns from my throat to my belly.

I wish it hadn't. I feel like I swallowed a car. My throat burns. I swallow again, not realizing until too late that my mouth is full of something other than spit.

The flavor changes. The old refrigerator smell dissolves into something hotter, more metallic. A desperate thirst presses hard against my chest, and I drink deeply, desperate to quench the fire, but it only serves to spread it.

I have fingers. They're wrapped tightly around something that feels like paper-wrapped steak. My toes are back too, and there's a drumming in my head, slow and steady and utterly maddening.

Thud, thud-thud, thud, thud-thud.

A heartbeat.

I can't tell if it's mine.

My eyes fly open to meet Tyresius's. His open wrist is in my mouth, filling me with his toxic blood. I break away, coughing and sputtering, trying to throw up. My throat hurts, my neck hurts, my belly hurts, and that godforsaken throbbing in my head just won't stop.

Tyresius fades away out of sight, but not before I catch the smug grin on his face.

I don't have time to be upset about what just

happened. There's no room for emotions left in my body. There's only room for pain.

The fire in my belly is spreading, consuming me cell by cell. If the pain came in waves, maybe I could deal with that, but it doesn't. It's slow, constant, and building. I can't see through the tears, and I can't hear over the sound of my own screams, but I can tell when I'm picked up and moved.

Every touch is agony.

Every jostling step makes me wish for death.

I've never been more relieved to be dumped on a cold, damp cement floor before. A heavy door locks behind me, and then I'm alone—just me and the endless, ceaseless pain.

CHAPTER TWENTY-FIVE

I don't know how much time passes.

The change sweeps through me like cold hunger, like a feverish glacier. Sweat freezes on my skin only to melt away again as a fresh wave consumes me. I hear things, but the sounds are all either indistinct or too sharp, and I can't make sense of any of them.

I smell food.

No, not food—people.

No, water.

Or steak.

It all seems to be one scent, but I don't know what it means anymore. Then my own sweaty stench overwhelms everything else and I'm alone again, deaf, blind, and helpless, isolated in my pain.

I've heard that childbirth and broken femurs are the most painful things humans can experience, because everything worse kills the nerve endings or the person before the brain can register anything else. I've never given birth, but I broke my femur once getting thrown from a horse.

It hurt, but it was nothing compared to this.

The walls seem to expand and then close in, pulsing in time to my agony. They're plain, earth-stained stone walls, black from three feet up to the floor. Sometimes the black part smells like blood and pain and terror. Sometimes it smells like shit.

Right now, all I can smell is a man—a clean man.

Part of me recognizes him, but not the part that's on speaking terms with my brain at the moment.

He's coming closer, and I have the sudden urge to find a long wooden stick. A sharp one. Fury explodes in my head that I can't find a stick and couldn't move to look for one even if I wanted to. The anger is followed by a wave of confused frustration as my free-wheeling mind struggles to latch on to anything that makes sense.

What do I need a stick for? Why am I even here?

The wall in front of me moves, but this is different than the strange pulsing movements I'm used to. After a few seconds, my addled mind pieces together that it's not the wall that's moving. It's the door, and it's opening.

Blinking hard, I force the small room I'm locked in to come into better focus. One of the walls, the one with the door in it, is made of thick metal bars. The other three are stone. I'm sprawled out on the floor, and from this vantage point, I can see two feet approaching me.

Someone is here to see me. But why?

What else could the vampires possibly do to me?

I struggle to stand up, but the room tilts before I even reach my knees. I pitch sideways, landing hard on one hip.

Bracing my upper body on my hands, I press against a floor that seems to want to run from my touch. I suck in a few deep breaths, wondering why the person who opened the door hasn't said anything yet. I can smell him, but like everything else, the scent doesn't make any sense to me at first. It isn't until I raise my eyes to look at him that it all clicks into place.

"Bas... Bastian," I breathe. My words are slurred and come out in a whimper.

Something changes around his eyes, but I can't tell if he's pleased or concerned. I pull myself together and force my gaze to meet his, anchoring myself to his eyes.

"Bastian, please. I... don't... want this."

His face doesn't change, but one of his hands curls into a fist.

Yes, hit me. Hit me hard enough to break my neck and kill me before the change makes it harder. Before it becomes almost impossible.

But I don't think his gesture is aimed at me. He's holding tightly to his self-control. I don't know what brought him down here, whether it was pure curiosity or the urge to gloat at my discomfort, but I'm hoping I can convince him to finish me off. He's a killer by nature, after all.

"Help me," I plead, the words coming out harshly through my raw throat. "Kill—me. I can't be—*this*."

There's a flash in his eye, a glint of anger.

Shit. I've offended him, dammit.

I can't afford to offend him. I need him. He needs to understand why I can't live like this. No, that's wrong. "Live" isn't even the right word. I'm already dead. I can't come back, not from the kinds of injuries Tyresius gave me when he tore into me. Not from that much blood loss.

There are only two options in front of me now.

Oblivion or eternity.

I grope around inside my addled mind for what to say, some way to bargain for the right to my own death. I need Bastian to *see* me, just like I see him.

"You told me that the thing you remember most is your parents being slaughtered in front of you by vampire hunters," I tell him quietly. My voice has grown stronger. That should be a good thing, but I know what it means. It won't be long now before my mouth sprouts fangs, and I become the one thing in the world I hate the most. I suck in a breath, but it doesn't help.

"I know what that feels like," I continue, my voice shaking.

Bastion frowns at me, the offended look on his face deepening.

I shake my head. "You don't believe me, but it's true. My parents were torn apart. Drained dry. They were killed by vampires while I watched through the slats in the closet. I was a child, Bastian. Barely old enough to understand what I was seeing." I laugh bitterly, choking a little on the air that rattles from my lungs. "So you see—we have something in common. Losing the people we love to violence and not being able to do anything about it."

He takes half a step into the small dungeon cell, and I realize that tears are streaming down my face.

"I couldn't save them," I rasp, my throat closing around my words. "I couldn't save Nathan." I look up at the tall, coldly beautiful man before me, pleading with everything in me. "But *you* can save *me*. You can keep me from doing any more harm. Please, Bastian—don't let me be both of our worst nightmares."

There's a hint of pain in the prince's eyes as he comes a little closer. He's hesitant, tentative, almost like he's afraid of me. I want to throw myself at him, want to scream and cry and force him to do what I ask. But I swallow it all back. I can see him thinking, can feel his resolve weakening. A sharp pain slices through my gums, traveling up to my eyes, and I cry out.

"Not long now," I choke out, pressing my palm over my

mouth. "Please. *Please*. Kill me. Quickly, before I forget why I need to die."

He hesitates for a moment longer, just out of reach. His eyes hold storms in them, and although his body isn't moving at all, there's nothing *still* about him. Then, finally, he sighs and nods, stepping toward me.

I brace myself for attack, my survival instinct flaring despite what I just begged him to do. I hope it's quick, whatever it is. A snapped neck would be good. Bleeding out wasn't too bad, but I don't know if it will work now that I have Tyresius's vampiric blood in my system. The bruises on my arms are already fading.

But Bastian doesn't grab me or strike. He doesn't twist my neck or crush my skull. Instead, he puts a small flask up to my lips.

"Drink," he murmurs hoarsely. "This will end it."

I do. I clutch at his arm and drink greedily, clinging to him as I tilt my head up to reach the flask better.

The liquid is bitter and pungent, thick enough to feel like wool in my mouth, but I force it all down. It tastes like death, which makes sense. I open my eyes after I empty the flask, and the edges of my vision have already gone dark. Bastian's warm, sad eyes are all I can focus on.

He pulls me into his arms, cradling me close and stroking my hair. His touch is tender, even though his chiseled features are still set in a mask.

"Thank you," I whisper quietly as the feeling runs out

of my fingers and toes.

I rub my face against his shirt, breathing in his scent. He doesn't ask what I'm thanking him for, and I'm glad. Even now, at the end, I have too much pride to tell someone that I'm grateful they took pity on me. I always thought I'd go out stronger than that.

"For death," I say instead, pushing the words past my lips even as my lungs begin to give out. "For letting me go. Thank you for... proving me wrong about you."

He kisses the top of my head, ignoring the fact that the strands must be crusted and tangled with blood and sweat. I tilt my head back so I can look into his beautiful storm-gray eyes one last time. With numb hands, I reach up to pull him down to me, threading my fingers through the silky hair at the back of his head.

I don't know why I do it, exactly.

I'm grateful, but that isn't the whole of it.

All I know for sure is that the last thing I want to do before I die is kiss Bastian.

His lips meet mine, and he kisses me back with more feeling than I expected. It feels like a goodbye kiss, just like Rome's did, full of unsaid words that neither of us will ever get to say now.

His arms crush me close, but soon, I stop feeling them. I stop feeling anything except his mouth, then I stop feeling that too.

My eyelids fall shut as the world goes black.

CHAPTER TWENTY-SIX

I've never been dead before, but I'm surprised it feels like *this*.

My skin is cool. I'm pressed against something rough, and it takes me a moment to realize that I'm lying on my back.

It takes me even longer to realize that I'm... breathing.

Every movie I've ever seen where someone is buried alive rushes through my head all at once, and I panic, breaking out in a cold sweat. I force my eyes open, expecting to see the inside of a coffin a few inches from my face. Instead, there's just the rebar-crossed concrete ceiling of the lowest level.

I'm in the same dark, dingy dungeon cell. Someone took the time to lay me on the flimsy cot in the corner, but I'm definitely still here.

I sit up and close my mouth, which has been hanging

open. I instantly regret it as I bite my lip. I don't bite it hard, but even so, blood wells up around my teeth. I lick my lip, then lick it again. The blood tastes... good.

It tastes like blood, but it's making me salivate.

Confused, I lick my lip again.

This time, I scrape my tongue against the offending teeth—newcomers in my mouth, sharp and vicious and unwieldy.

Fangs.

No.

No, no, no. Please, no.

"That son of a bitch," I growl. My voice is hoarse, giving out before I even finish the words, but I don't know if that's because my throat is still ragged from all the screaming I did earlier, or because I can't seem to find my breath.

I can't breathe. A kind of horror is washing through me that I've never experienced before, something that seems to creep into my bones and chill them from the inside out. I've only felt like this once before, and it was the day I watched helplessly as my parents died.

I should've died today.

This should've been over.

"Goddammit," I whisper brokenly.

I want to be furious at Bastian for betraying me, I really do, and I will be... as soon as I'm done being heartbroken over it. I really thought he took pity on me. I thought I could make him understand.

But he lied to me.

Whatever I drank, whatever was in that flask, it was clearly never meant to kill me. Instead, it just knocked me unconscious for the last bit of the change.

Even though we never even spent that much time together, Bastian clearly knows me well. I'm used to fighting. If he had fought me, I would have forced him to kill me, even in my weakened state.

But he beat me with the one thing I could never fight against—tenderness.

And now I'll have the rest of my very long life to regret it.

ACKNOWLEDGMENTS

Alice Best, thank you for helping me find the perfect name for my heroine!

BOOKS BY CALLIE ROSE

Boys of Oak Park Prep
Savage Royals
Defiant Princess
Broken Empire

Kings of Linwood Academy
The Help
The Lie
The Risk

Ruthless Games
Sweet Obsession
Sweet Retribution
Sweet Salvation

Fallen University

Year One
Year Two
Year Three

Claimed by Wolves
Fated Magic
Broken Bond
Dark Wolf
Alpha Queen

Feral Shifters
Rejected Mate
Untamed Mate
Cursed Mate
Claimed Mate

Kingdom of Blood
Blood Debt
Dark Legacy
Vampire Wars

Printed in Great Britain
by Amazon